I0642201

Mortimer Collins, F. Percy Cotton

Selections from the poetical works

Mortimer Collins, F. Percy Cotton

Selections from the poetical works

ISBN/EAN: 9783337275464

Printed in Europe, USA, Canada, Australia, Japan

Cover: Foto ©Andreas Hilbeck / pixelio.de

More available books at **www.hansebooks.com**

SELECTIONS

FROM

THE POETICAL WORKS

OF

MORTIMER COLLINS

MADE BY

F. PERCY COTTON

LONDON

RICHARD BENTLEY & SON, NEW BURLINGTON ST.

Publishers in Ordinary to Her Majesty the Queen

1886

TO MY COUSIN

FRANCES

WIDOW OF MORTIMER COLLINS

I DEDICATE THIS BOOK

PREFACE.

FOR the last ten years I have occupied much of
my leisure time in putting music to Mortimer
Collins' lyrics, and I have thus become familiar
with the poet's works.

I discovered that many of the best poems
were scattered about in magazines and newspapers, and therefore likely to be lost; so I
have made it a labour of love, from time to time,
to collect all these.

In putting together this volume my only
difficulty has been to know what choice to
make from such a wealth of material. I had
intended at first to include only those pieces

which had not hitherto been collected; but, finding that Mortimer Collins' previous volumes of verse — namely, *Idylls and Rhymes*, 1855; *Summer Songs*, 1860; *The Inn of ·Strange Meetings*, 1870,—were all out of print, I thought well to reproduce a few of the best poems from those volumes.

Having access to the poet's papers, I have been fortunate in finding some pieces that have not yet been published, from which I have chosen a few.

It has often been asked who wrote the *Comedy of Dreams*, and where the book could be found. The work lived only in Mortimer Collins' brain, intended, no doubt, to be produced at some time when the pressing necessities of life were less upon him; but fragments of it were occasionally written down, merely to serve as mottoes for the chapters of his novels. I have arranged these fragments in the best way I could to show some thread of story running through. I am sure many persons will agree with me that, disjointed as they are, they were worth collecting.

The *Letter to Disraeli* was published anonymously, in pamphlet form, in 1869, but attracted no notice; and the surplus copies were, I believe, sold as waste-paper.

It is generally considered that a poet does his best work while he is young, but I think any one acquainted with Mortimer Collins' works must acknowledge that he improved with age. The greater part of the pieces in this volume were written after he was forty. He died when he had just completed his forty-ninth year, and, to judge from his later work, he was but just reaching his full mental power.

Those who know the lady to whom this volume is dedicated [the F. C. to whom several of the poems are addressed] will understand why Mortimer Collins' poetical faculties developed during the last decade of his life.

F. PERCY COTTON.

PINE TREE HILL,

CAMBERLEY, SURREY,

February 1886.

CONTENTS.

TO MY WIFE.[1]

Fair, my own darling, are the flowers of Spring. . . .
Rathe primrose, violet, and eglantine,
Anemone and golden celandine :
Not less delicious all the birds that sing
Carols of joy upon the amorous wing,
Earine, in these sweet hours of thine.
Spring's youngest sister art thou, Lady mine,

Child who hast love for every living thing
Of earth and air.   A moment now I linger—
Linger, and think of thee, and give thee this
Love-gift of rhymes made when my spirit was free.
If thou wilt touch it with a white forefinger—
Nay, if the volume thou wilt deign to kiss—
Surely my song shall live, Earine.

[1] Dedication of a previous volume of Poems.

B

TO F. C.

FAST falls the snow, O lady mine,
Sprinkling the lawn with crystals fine,
But by the gods we won't repine
    While we're together,
We'll chat and rhyme and kiss and dine,
    Defying weather.

So stir the fire and pour the wine,
And let those sea-green eyes divine
Pour their love-madness into mine :
    I don't care whether
'Tis snow or sun or rain or shine
    If we're together.

A CONCEIT.

O TOUCH that rosebud ! it will bloom—
    My lady fair !
A passionate red in dim green gloom,
A joy, a splendour, a perfume   ·
    That breathes in air.

You touched my heart ; it gave a thrill
    Just like a rose
That opens at a lady's will ;
Its bloom is always yours until
    You bid it close.

3

I AND MY SWEETHEART.

I AND my sweetheart spelt together ;
  Our ages were together ten :
How sad to waste the sweet spring weather
  In the old Dame's fusty den !
White lilac, fragrant, graceful, cool,
Tapped at the window of the school :
Alas, too well our doom we knew—
There was a tremulous birch-tree too.

I and my sweetheart dwell together :
  Many tens are our ages now :
Vanished is youth's gay violet weather,
  Stays the old Dame's frowning brow.
Dame Nature keeps the eternal school,
And grows keen twigs to flog the fool ;
But looks away, with pardoning eye,
When we play truant, my love and I.

LOVE.

WHAT'S the use of living in
   Such a world as this is,
Where they say that love's a sin,
   Deep in sin's abysses?

Toil and strive, and thereby thrive,
   Shun whate'er is sunny :
If you're fool enough to wive,
   Mind you marry money.

May the God who made the sun,
   Trees, birds, woman's beauty,
Scourge the fools who have begun
   Thus to teach men duty.

While my lady's heart's astir,
   'Neath its milk-white cover,
All the birds shall sing of her,
   All who see shall love her.

5

VIOLETS AT HOME.

I.

O HAPPY buds of violet !
I give them to my sweet, and she
Puts them where something sweeter yet
Must always be.

II.

White violets find whiter rest :
For fairest flowers how fair a fate !
For me remain, O fragrant breast !
Inviolate.

6

"MY LADY SINGS."

ALL through the day, O happy thrush !
I hear thy music's torrent gush ;
Then comes the blackbird's mellower flute,
And merrily when both are mute
                    The robin sings :
But when the blue turns golden-pale,
Hist ! there's a strange impassioned tale
Told by the Daulian nightingale
                    With dusky wings.

O magic music, linger still !
Echo, from the furze-clad hill,
Tosses back with semblance fine
The dreamy ecstacy divine,
                    And ether rings :
But lo, through windows open wide
To catch the breath of eventide,
Comes lovelier sound than aught beside—
                    My lady sings.

SONNET TO F. C.

WOMEN there are who say the world is slow
  To recognise their scientific power ;
  Wherefore they fill with heat the flying hour,
And let the beauty of their sweet life go
Like water thro' a child's frail fingers. So
  Might the tree murmur not to be a tower,
  Might envy of the strong storm vex the shower
That wakes sweet blossoms and makes brooklets
  flow.
The lady whom I love has no such thought ;
  No stolid strength of mind shall make her weak,
  No folly sink her in the sad abyss
Where these same scientific souls are caught.
  She knows a kiss befits a lovely cheek,
Ay, and that rosy lips were made to kiss.

DAWN.

DAWN, with flusht foot upon the mountain-tops,
  Stands beckoning to the Sun-god's golden car,
  While on her high clear brow the morning star
Grows fainter, as the silver-misty copse
    And rosy river-bend and village white
      Feel the strong shafts of light.

The tide of dreams has reached its utter ebb ;
  The joy of Dawn is in my Lady's eyes,
  Where at her window with a half-surprise
She sees the meadows meshed with fairy web,
    And hears the happy skylark far above,
      Singing, *I live ! I love !*

THE KING AND THE BEGGAR MAID.

A NEW READING.

THE young King stands by his palace-gate,
 O what a joy is the youth of a King!
Tired a little of splendour and state—
 Hark in the valley the sweet birds sing.

Like a lion's mane his yellow hair,
 His eye as keen as a hawk's on the wing,
The ladies gaze and tremble there—
 Ah, is it not sweet, the love of a King?

He sees the towers of his city below,
 O shining river! O ships that swing!
Through wide white streets his people flow,
 Hark, the bells of the Minster ring!

The Beggar comes by with a nut-brown skin,
 Ah, deep in the heart lies misery's sting!
Her eye has a blue to the sky akin,
 Tirra-lirra, he hears her sing.

Forward he strides as the girl he sees,
O how wild is the will of a King !
The ladies titter under the trees ;
Still the bells of the Minster ring.

What the young King whispers none has heard,
Hey for the heath where the wild birds sing !
But the echo is caught of the Beggar's word :
" I love my love, and he is not a King."

A BIRTHDAY LETTER TO F. C.

14TH JULY 1875.

AH, where was I, that happy day
My pretty —— came this way?
Surely the careless wandering boy
Felt in his heart a thrill of joy,
Saw in the sky a brighter gleam,
Had, as he stroll'd, a mystic dream
Of the fair child of wit and whim
That very moment born for him.
    I don't know where, I don't know how,
      But I will swear that I
    Recorded a true marriage-vow
      In that July.

She came into the world for me:
I wonder if the summer sea

Whisper'd of her an amorous tale—
Or if the dulcet nightingale
Utter'd through the woods a word
Of the cooing little bird,
Just flown down from spheres divine,
To be mine, yes, always mine.
   I care not how, I care not who,
     Brought tidings from the sky,
     But I will swear my bride I knew
     In that July.

I knew her, yes, no matter how,
Even as I know her now—
A goddess with two loving eyes,
A baby that was born too wise.

   .   .   .   .

A lady who, in happiest mood,
Could teach the world of Ladyhood,
   Since now she came to earth's green coast,
     Among the months shall I
     Revere the most (and kiss her most
     Therein) July.

P.S.

I often think, my only love,
  The world would be more true,
If half the ladies in the world
  Were half as good as you.

And don't you think, my only love,
  'Twere merrier 'neath the sky,
If half the men in half the world
  Could love as well as I ?

THE IVORY GATE.

Sunt geminæ Somni portæ : quarum altera fertur
Cornea ; qua veris facilis datur exitus umbris :
Altera candenti perfecta nitens elephanto ;
Sed falsa ad cœlum mittunt insomnia Manes.

VIRGIL.

I.

WHEN, loved by poet and painter
    The sunrise fills the sky,
When night's gold urns grow fainter,
    And in depths of amber die—
When the morn-breeze stirs the curtain,
    Bearing an odorous freight—
Then visions strange, uncertain,
    Pour thick through the Ivory Gate.

II.

Then the oars of Ithaca dip so
    Silently into the sea,

That they wake not sad Calypso—
And the Hero wanders free :
He breasts the ocean-furrows,
    At war with the words of Fate—
And the blue tide's low susurrus
    Comes up to the Ivory Gate.

III.

Or, clad in the hide of leopard,
    'Mid Ida's freshest dews,
Paris, the Teucrian shepherd,
    His sweet Œnone woos :
On the thought of her coming bridal
    Unuttered joy doth wait—
While the tune of the false one's idyl
    Rings soft through the Ivory Gate.

IV.

Or down from green Helvellyn
    The roar of streams I hear,
And the lazy sail is swelling
    To the winds of Windermere :

That girl with the rustic bodice
'Mid the ferry's laughing freight
Is as fair as any goddess
    Who sweeps through the Ivory Gate.

V.

Ah, the vision of dawn is leisure—
But the truth of day is toil :
And we pass from dreams of pleasure
    To the world's unstayed turmoil.
Perchance, beyond the river
    Which guards the realms of Fate,
Our spirits may dwell for ever
    'Mong dreams of the Ivory Gate.

C

MY THRUSH.

I.

ALL through the sultry hours of June,
From morning blithe to golden noon,
  And till the star of evening climbs
The gray-blue East, a world too soon,
  There sings a Thrush amid the limes.

II.

God's poet, hid in foliage green,
Sings endless songs, himself unseen ;
  Right seldom come his silent times.
Linger, ye summer hours serene !
  Sing on, dear Thrush, amid the limes!

III.

May I not dream God sends thee there,
Thou mellow angel of the air,
  Even to rebuke my earthlier rhymes

With music's soul, all praise and prayer?
Is that thy lesson in the limes?

IV.

Closer to God art thou than I:
His minstrel thou, whose brown wings fly
Through silent æther's sunnier climes.
Ah, never may thy music die!
Sing on, dear Thrush, amid the limes!

AD CHLOEN, M.A.

(Fresh from her Cambridge Examination.)

I.

LADY, very fair are you,
And your eyes are very blue,
     And your hose ;
And your brow is like the snow,
And the various things you know
     Goodness knows.

II.

And the rose-flush on your cheek,
And your algebra and Greek
     Perfect are ;
And that loving lustrous eye
Recognises in the sky
     Every star.

III.

You have pouting piquant lips,
You can doubtless an eclipse
   Calculate ;
But for your cærulean hue,
I had certainly from you
   Met my fate.

IV.

If by an arrangement dual
I were Adams mixed with Whewell,
   Then some day
I, as wooer, perhaps might come
To so sweet an Artium
   Magistra.

CHLOE, M.A.

AD AMANTEM SUUM.

I.

CARELESS rhymer, it is true
That my favourite colour's blue :
      But am I
To be made a victim, sir,
If to puddings I prefer
      Cambridge π ?

II.

If with giddier girls I play
Croquet through the summer day
      On the turf,
Then at night ('tis no great boon)
Let me study how the moon
      Sways the surf.

III.

TENNYSON'S idyllic verse
Surely suits me none the worse
   If I seek
Old Sicilian birds and bees—
Music of sweet SOPHOCLES—
   Golden Greek.

IV.

You have said my eyes are blue ;
There may be a fairer hue,
   Perhaps—and yet
It is surely not a sin
If I keep my secrets in
   Violet.

A POET'S PHILOSOPHY.

I.

A SAFFRON crescent in an opal sky
He watched—while she into her wine-dark hair
Braided white violets—whiter than despair,
And half as sweet as love. There fluttered by
Wings of the merle, gay caroller, who sleeps
Upon a beechen bough in the far forest deeps.

II.

This cottage on the mighty forest-verge
Was placed : primeval woodland, where the deer
But seldom might the huntsman's bugle hear.
The great oaks thundered like the ocean-surge
When came a tempest. Alpine hills afar
Caught in the crimson east the lustrous evening
star.

-

III.

More of the Garden than the Portico
    Was his philosophy who dwelt therein.
    He was not fain 'mid the mad world to win
Power or renown from the sparse overflow
    Of Fortune's horn.   To him three things were
    fair—
True Love, unfettered Song, and the wooing
    Summer air.

IV.

That wooing air that wiles the red rose forth
    To fling its passionate fragrance everywhere—
    To lay its crimson heart all torn and bare
On Summer's altar.   Not the bitter north,
    Keen-cutting as an Arab scimitar,
But that which feels the touch of Sirius, scorching
    star.

V.

That wild free song which will not wear a fetter,
    Such as was mastered.well by loving Shelley
    (Pure poet, down-ridden in the world's hot *mêlée*),

Or such as Shakespeare uttered, careless setter
  In Orient gold of perfect amethysts,
Whom men must marvel at, while the great world
  exists.

VI.

That absolute love which many women feel,
  But men how few !   Not winds which icily
  Breathe freshness underneath a twilight sky,
When swift Apollo's burning chariot-wheel
  Flies westward, bear to mortals such delight
As that most perfect love, unselfish, infinite.

VII.

Without it, marble-templed cities reaching
  Long piers into the sea were but as dens
  For untamed beasts — as most unwholesome
  fens,
Stagnant and damp.   Without it, the beseeching
  Bosom of Nature, whereon poets lie,
Were but a cromlech gaunt, on which men well
  might die.

VIII.

With it, the air we breathe intoxicates
  Our spirits with unceasing glee : the sky
  Rains music from its blue immensity ;
Rhyme, rhyme immortal on our utterance waits ;
  No end, no efflux of our joy can come—
For we are demigods, and earth's Elysium.

.   .   .   .

φιλυμνος, φιλυπνος.

IX.

Lo, song and sleep I love.   For song's susurrus
  Is the soul's wine throughout the weary days :
  And silent sleep, restorer of decays,
Smooths from the fretted brow the deepening
    furrows ;
  'Tis the true Fountain of Jouvence, unfound
By knight or troubadour in the far forest ground.

X.

Anacreon's tettix, singing in the trees,
  Unworn by age, and like the gods therein—
Or the amorous thrush, that does at dawn begin,
Nor ceases till there's sunset on the seas :
  These are the lords of melody, for whom
Earth has no touch of sadness, death no dream
  of doom.

XI.

But we have mortal form, material tissue ;
  And as the heavy centuries come and go,
  Closer the clay clings, wearier human woe,
Fewer the lips wherefrom true song may issue.
  More sluggishly the poet's pulses stir
Than when the gay Greek wore the golden grass-
  hopper.

XII.

And yet, Earine, do violets white
  In thy sweet season kiss the wooing south ;
  Still hath the cyclamen its ruddy mouth,

And five fine petals made of liquid light :
Still at the early dawn's delicious burst
A myriad tawny throats their music have dispersed.

XIII.

Death is the ocean of immortal rest :
And what is sleep ?   A bath our Angel brings
Of the same lymph, fed by the self-same springs:
Dip in it, and freshen the despondent breast,
   And taste the salt breath of the great wide sea,
Where shines 'mid laughing waves a far-off isle
   for me.

XIV.

Why fear ?   The light wind whitens all the brine,
   And throws fresh foam upon the marble shores,
   Or it may be that strong and strenuous oars
Must force the shallop o'er the hyaline :
   But welcome utter calm or bitter blast—
The voyage will be done, the island reached at
   last.

XV.

O the precipitous cliffs, the amber sand,
 The drowsy valleys musical with brooks,
 Asphodel glimmering in shadowy nooks,
Far slopes of virgin turf where oak trees stand
 Which in forgotten cycles Rhaicos knew
Ere her maimed messenger to the Hamadryad flew.

XVI.

If we are weak with immemorial strife,
 If sadder destiny each æra weaves,
 Yet listen to the lyrics 'mid the leaves,
Look to the life beyond the verge of life.
 Let the dull lecture and the womanish weep :
To the Poet leave the wine of song, the realm of
 sleep.

நதி," *We are such stuff*
As dreams are made on, and our little life
Is rounded with a sleep."

XVII.

Dew on the lawns, and fragrance of fresh flowers,
And magical song of mellow-throated birds—
A beauty untransmutable to words :
Such is the vision of the morning hours ;
When fade the urns of night in saffron skies,
And light and love return to young dream-haunted
    eyes.

XVIII.

Earine has sucked the breath of Spring—
And I have touched thy lips, Earine,
What time the Dawn came from the purple sea,
And forests fluttered to the waving wing
Of the unwearying Angel who doth sweep
Back upon heavy hinge the porphyry gates of sleep.

XIX.

Delicious thus to enter Morning Land :
The world is wondrous, for the world is new ;

Dim drosera is all o'erdrenched with dew.
Ah, well might Merlin wake in Broceliande,
And see the daybreak through the oaks that wave
Where ivy and violet grow on his melodious grave.

XX.

Will it be thus when the strange sleep of death
Lifts from the brow, and lost eyes live again ?
Will Morning dawn on the bewildered brain
To cool and heal ?   And shall I feel the breath
Of freshening winds that travel from the sea,
And meet thy loving laughing eyes, Earine ?

XXI.

Is life a dream, and death a sleep, and love
The only thing immortal ?   Who would care
To be received into the ambient air,
Or traverse æther like a cloud, above
The happy homes of mortals ?   Must the soul
Be formlessly absorbed into the infinite whole ?

XXII.

No : I shall pass into the Morning Land
As now from sleep into the life of morn ;

Live the new life of the new world, unshorn
Of the swift brain, the executing hand ;
See the dense darkness suddenly withdrawn,
As when Orion's sightless eyes discerned the dawn.

XXIII.

I shall behold it : I shall see the utter
  Glory of sunrise heretofore unseen,
  Freshening the woodland ways with brighter
    green,
And calling into life all wings that flutter,
  All throats of music and all eyes of light,
And driving o'er the verge the intolerable night.

XXIV.

O virgin world ! O marvellous far days !
  No more with dreams of grief doth love grow
    bitter,
  Nor trouble dim the lustre wont to glitter
In happy eyes.   Decay alone decays :
  A moment—death's dull sleep is o'er ; and we
Drink the immortal morning air, Earine.

.   .   ,   .   .

D

" Si mihi Nausicaë patrios concederet hortos,
Alcinoö possem dicere, *Malo meos*."

XXV.

Immortal gardens of the island King,
  Set in bright æther of the Odyssey,
  With bloom and fruitage on the self-same tree,
Scaturient fountains always murmuring
  Through odorous cyclamen and hyacinth,
While roses flush around the marble palace-plinth.

XXVI.

Delicious dream !   What if Nausikaa came—
  The white-armed delicate-ankled Princess who
  To the river led her maiden retinue
And found the Hero—saying, with virgin shame
  On royal cheek, " O stranger from the sea,
Rest from thy wandering ! Take these : take also me."

XXVII.

Rome's brilliant rascal-epigrammatist
  Preferred his Spanish gardens.   Likewise I,
  Having found my Princess 'neath a grayer sky,
Think England's sunshine, windy rain, white mist,

Turf like the emerald, touched with crocus-fire,
Lovelier than that Greek dream, whose calm would
  surely tire.

XXVIII.

Some thirty miles from Megalopolis,
  Miles also from the shrieking griding rail,
  On a high road where once the four-horse mail
Flashed gaily past—so placed my cottage is :
  Roars merrily now the wind tall limes between,
Which guard my quiet lawn, a triangle scalene.

XXIX.

And you may see me, if you pass this way,
  Lean on my gate and look into the road,
  And listen to the skylark's joyous ode—
Thoughtful, not oft cigarless.   Will you say,
  "Who wears that velvet coat, a trifle tattered,
That curious cool straw hat, which wind and rain
  have battered ? "

XXX.

Sometimes there comes a friendly visitant,
  Brimmed with the life o' the town, rewarding me

Well for my mutton and my Burgundy ;
And so we laugh together at fraud and cant,
　While everywhere is heard a flutter of wings,
And winter's chorister, the unwearying redbreast,
　sings.

XXXI.

O, but one visitant, the nightingale !
　Throb, throb, wild voice, through passionate
　　twilight hours !
　Love is thy gift from the Eternal Powers ;
Yet in thy song there seems a tragic wail,
　Because in Argos, ages long ago,
A poet turned thy lyric wooing into woe.

XXXII.

Truly the poet is omnipotent :
　His magic alters melody of birds,
　Puts life, love, glory, into dead cold words,
Conjures all angels 'neath the gray sky's tent,
　Bathes common things in light Hesperian. Thus
My garden I prefer to yours, Alcinoüs.

ON WINDERMERE.

I.

DROOP, droop, soft little eyelids !
Droop over eyes of weird wild blue !
Under the fringe of those tremulous shy lids
Glances of love and of fun peep through.

II.

Sing, sing, sweetest of maidens !
Carol away with thy white little throat !
Echo awakes to the exquisite cadence,
Here on the magical mere afloat.

III.

Dream, dream, heart of my own love !
Sweet is the wind from the odorous south—
Sweet is the island we sail to alone, love—
Sweet is a kiss from thy ruddy young mouth.

CHARLES LAMB'S CENTENARY.

"February 10 is the centenary of the birthday of Charles Lamb. It is thought that this offers a fit opportunity to establish some memorial of him in his old school, where, I am ashamed to say, no visible trace of him exists."—*Letter of* G. C. BELL (*Head-Master of Christ's Hospital*) *in the* "*Times.*"

DEAR ELIA, born a hundred years ago,
How through and through your quiet life we know :
How we delight in those quaint essays, made
Out of soul-sunlight conquering life-shade :
How we enjoy your happy style, sore sated
Of large words with but little meaning weighted :
How every one who reads your prose or rhymes,
Feels to you as a comrade of those times,
That heard you pun and stammer out your joke,
And breathed the fragrance of your curling smoke:
For never reader could your Essays end,
Without the thought, " Dear ELIA is my friend ! "

Now the Head-Master of that famous school,
Where once you writhed 'neath flagellating rule,
And, when birch-rod produced accordant hymn,
Envied unpunishable cherubim,
Writes to the *Times*—says briefly, " Let us do
Something for that dear ancient brilliant Blue."
Punch says the same, for through the world who
    knows
So exquisite a master of sweet prose,
So beautiful a dreamer, though the sky
To which you soared was not immensely high ;
So subtle an observer of all things
Kindly and quaint, with old-world colourings.
What though the playful fancies of your pen
Be your memorial in the hearts of Men,
'Tis sad to know, where a boy-blue you played,
Within the churchyard where your bones are laid,
Your grave neglected,[1] and your schoolroom wall,
Without a stone your memory to recall !

[1] See letter of Mr. Percy Fitzgerald in the *Daily News*,
Saturday, February 13.

LORD CARNARVON, in his Speech at the Literary Fund
Dinner in 1876, said he doubted whether those who
wrote much were happy.

WHY in the world should the question arise ?
Is the course that bright-winged Pegasus flies
    To be measured by means mechanic ?
There's a power and passion that urge to write,
And the energy fills with strong delight,
That moves the natural easy might
    Of a genius Titanic.

As the war-horse neighs in the battle-hour,
So the spirit of fire, the wielder of power,
    Works on, and in strength rejoices.
Better his visions than fortune or fame ;
To spend himself is his glorious aim ;
He can wait for Posterity's sure acclaim,
    If grudged the multitude's voices.

The fickle taste of the thoughtless town
May wrongly assign the laurel crown :
     Why should that spoil life's flavour ?
Destiny works on a curious plan,
And is often kind to the charlatan ;
But the man who has power is the happy man,
     Whoever has Fortune's favour.

A PORTRAIT.

Lo ! in his easy chair behold the Master,
   While shade and sunlight race athwart the lawn,
A man who undismayed beholds disaster,
   Nor fears the midnight though he loves the
   dawn.
On him the very elements seem to fawn,
   And all wild creatures : sunlight follows him,
Winds cool him, and the wild birds' notes are
   drawn
   Out into music for him, when the dim
Long alleys of the wood in mist of twilight swim.

TRUE DELIGHT.

I.

To dwell amid the lime-leaves' sweet susurrus—
      O true delight !
To toil in dreary towns for guerdon sordid—
      O cursed spite !
Of me be this one happiness recorded
That care for gold my forehead never furrows :
      O true delight !

II.

With thoughts of Love I never can be lonely :
With Show and Noise existence waxeth bitter.
Mine are the carolling thrush, the rivulet's glitter,
Mine the soft solace of one bosom only,
      O true delight !

III.

Love is my source of power, my life's completeness:
The true delight !
Who will may be ambitious, avaricious.
Far-travelling thoughts are mine, and dreams
delicious,
And the sky's splendour and the rose's sweetness—
O true delight !

KANT ON THE MONTH OF FEBRUARY.

"O happy February! in which man has least to bear—
least pain, least sorrow, least self-reproach!"—*Diary of
Immanuel Kant.*

I.

TWELVE gems, the girdle of the year. . . .
     And every year
A name of joy or grief and fear;
Sometimes a creature sweet and soft,
A cruel demon very oft:
Seventy was wild with battle-thunder—
But what of Seventy-one, men wonder,
     A maiden year?

II.

Twelve gems. Ah, what, on mere and pond,
     Can shine beyond
December's icy diamond?

45

And lo the ruby red of June
With full-flushed rose and song-bird's tune !
April beholds the opal vary.
Dim amethyst to February
                    May well respond.

III.

A happy month.   Immanuel Kant,
                    Hierophant
Of the philosophy dominant,
Because its days are twenty-eight,
Welcomes it from the hand of Fate :
Least it contains of loves that languish,
Of dulness, agony, and anguish,
                    Swindling and cant.

IV.

Metaphysician !   I defy
                    This dreary dry
Month-preference; and I tell you why.
No stretch of time can be too long
For life's gay laugh and love's sweet song :
Add to each merry month a quarter. . . .
My love will only deem it shorter,
                    And so shall I.

WINTER IN BRIGHTON.

Vides, ut alta stet nive candidum
Soracte.

I.

WILL there be snowfall on lofty Soracte
After a summer so tranquil and torrid ?
Whoso detests the east wind, as a fact he
Thinks 'twill be horrid.
But there are zephyrs more mild by the ocean,
Every keen touch of the snowdrifts to lighten :
If to be cosy and snug you've a notion—
Winter in Brighton !

II.

Politics nobody cares about ; spurn a
Topic whereby all our happiness suffers.
Dolts in the back streets of Brighton return a
Couple of duffers.

47

Fawcett and White in the Westminster Hades
Strive the reporters' misfortunes to heighten.
What does it matter ?   Delicious young ladies
        Winter in Brighton !

III.

Good is the turtle for luncheon at Mutton's,
   Good is the hock that they give you at Bacon's,
Mainwaring's fruit in the bosoms of gluttons
        Yearning awakens.
Buckstone comes hither, delighting the million,
   'Mong the theatrical minnows a Triton ;
Dickens and Lemon pervade the pavilion :—
        Winter in Brighton !

IV.

If you've a thousand a year, or a minute—
   If you're a D'Orsay, whom every one follows—
If you've a head (it don't matter what's in it)
        Fair as Apollo's—
If you approve of flirtations, good dinners,
   Seascapes divine which the merry winds whiten,
Nice little saints and still nicer young sinners—
        Winter in Brighton !

THE SWAN AND THE POET.

A SWAN on Thames was gliding slow,
   While the heron fished and the swallow dipped
   And the willow-wands were emerald tipped ;
And deep in his heart was longing to know
What was his second self below :
   " 'Tis as white as I, and it swims like me—
Which, which can the real one be ? "

A Poet looked on his hero who
   Made a stir in the world with wooing and fight,
   Was the soul of war and the Court's delight,
Kissed red lips and a keen sword drew ;
And the Poet thought, " I wish I knew
   Whether this is another form of me,
   Whether this I have been or this shall be."

E

THE SWALLOW.

O SWALLOW, flying by windy ways,
   Over leagues of white sea-foam,
To the nest you left in the autumn days
   Under eaves of an English home—
Voyage right swiftly, wandering bird,
   A speck in the distant blue,
For the pulse of life in the leaves is stirred,
        And white doves coo.

II.

Have you wintered away in the Cyclades
   Or on marge of mysterious Nile?
No matter, so that the summer sees
   You back in our western isle.

But come, more swift than the sailing ship,
  For the skies are calm and clear,
And I long to see your brown wing dip
        In stream and mere.

III.

Yes, I long for the magic of indolent hours,
  The glamour of amorous eyes,
When the breeze which fluttered 'mid fern and flowers
  In the noon's rich langour dies,
When bees grow drowsy in honey-bells,
  And the brown lark sleeps in his nest,
And a vernal vision of gladness swells
        One soft white breast.

IV.

Yes, I long to float on a haunted lake,
  And the weary past forget,
And the thirst of my restless heart to slake
  With the songs of Amoret.
So, hither, swallow, from Memphian fane,
  Or Greek isle set in the blue :
Fly fast to your English home again—
        Love comes with you.

MAY.

May, like a girl at a garden gate
  With slender fingers lily-bells grasp,
With eyes of hazel that wonder and wait,
  And a hand that longs to lift the hasp,
Is sighing, " Ah, when will summer begin ?
When shall I open and let love in ? "

Mistress mine are you like May,
  The maiden month in her tender green,
Looking wistfully up the way
  Whence music is heard, whence summer is seen?
Will you lift the latch as my foot draws nigh
To your gate of love ? for I mean to try.

SONNET.

A WOMAN who is light from heart to eye,
    A woman who is love from eye to heart ;
    That is true beauty.   Ah, on life's rough chart
Mark down the place of meeting ere you die,
If you have met such woman.   Never sigh
    If she desire you to dwell far apart :
    Just to have made a vein of anger start
In her strong soul is something.   Ah, but why
Is it that such a woman seldom sees
    The man of calm imaginative brain,
The man who loves the birds and flowers and trees,
    Who fathoms pleasure and finds power in pain ?
One glance, one grasp, would make one flesh of
    these,
    Yet go they wandering round the world in
    vain.

MIDNIGHT SPECULATIONS.

I.

MY WIFE.

STRANGE : I sit here, and write my painful prose,
And my sweet love is in the Land of Dreams,
Where bloom weird flowers and murmur mystic
  streams,
And with wild wilful curve life's current flows,
So what will happen next no creature knows
  In that far region : some mad Demon seems
  To twist in puzzling knots the common themes
Of cheerful day.   Now, as her dear eyes close
Under fair lids that I have kissed so oft,
  Her spirit is a myriad leagues away
  Fast flitting o'er sea and land, or high in air
Borne by some wondrous witchery aloft.
  I want to travel on the self-same way :
  I want to follow and to find her there.

II.

MY DOG.

A mighty Pyrenean wolf-hound lies
  Beside me while I work or think or dream,
  And midnight passes like a mystic stream,
And in the icy blue of winter skies
Star after star grows wonderful and dies.
  To me those bright orbs yield no glory or gleam—
  Snug, curtained, and intent upon my theme—
Wrapt in myself.   Even so my great dog sighs,
Close at my feet, in visions of the chase
  Of wild wolves howling over hills of snow,
  Slain by his stalwart fathers long ago.
My thoughts within him find no resting-place :
  Of me he knows just what of him I know.
  Strange is the stern fate that hath made it so.

BIRDS AND LOVERS.

I.

O BROWN lark, loving cloud-land best
    And sunsmit seas of sky,
Thee does a musical unrest
Drive to rise upward from thy nest
        Far fathoms high.

II.

O fluid-fluting blackbird, keep
    The midnight of thy wing
Close to my home, where leaves grow deep,
Since where two lovers lie asleep
        Thou lovest to sing.

A ROBIN PERCHED ON A SUN-DIAL.

I.

THE robin sings on the dial,
　　For what knows he about time,
Red-breasted atom, whose life
　　Is only an endless trial
To out-do all rivals in strife
　　Of melody's silver chime.

II.

The shadow travelling slow
　　Is the lord of everything,
Terrible shortener of days.
　　But the sweet bird does not know—
He sings 'mid the summer haze,
　　In the wintriest cold he'll sing.

STRENGTH WITH AGE.

I HAVE been young and now am old :
    I then was weak, I now am strong.
Thus say I, as the sunset's gold
    Is poured the western skies along.

Weak was I, for I loved to see
    A pretty girl with blushing cheek,
And if the damsel smiled at me,
    I grew that minute twice as weak.

Weak was I, since I longed for fame,
    And if there dropt a ray oblique
Of sunshine on my boyish name,
    Why I was twenty times as weak.

Strong am I now : because the maid
    Who shall be lovely in these eyes
Must be no foolish flirting jade,
    But softly gay and simply wise.

Strong am I, since I cannot care
For fickle fancies of the throng,
But love to breathe Olympian air
With the disdainful God of Song.

The crowding years are gifts of gold ;
He wrongs himself whom Time can wrong.
I have been young and now am old :
I then was weak—I now am strong.

MULTUM IN PARVO.

A LITTLE shadow makes the sunrise sad,
    A little trouble checks the race of joy,
A little agony may drive men mad,
    A little madness may the soul destroy:
        Such is the world's annoy.

Ay, and the rose is but a little flower
    Which the red Queen of all the garden is:
And Love, which lasteth but a little hour,
    A moment's rapture and a moment's kiss,
        . Is what no man would miss.

"And they heard the voice of the Lord God walking in the garden in the cool of the day."—GENESIS iii. 8.

AH, the most ancient time,
When God and man were friends,
And earth was rounded with a summer clime,
And the dull doubt that lends
Sorrow to life was all a thing unknown.
Before those hours had flown
God walked at eventide thro' Eden's shade
And spoke to Man, and Man was not afraid.

Cannot that time return?
Is it not here, for those
Who from the strong still work of God can learn
His grandeur of repose?
A day with Him is as a myriad years,
A tear outweighs the spheres,
And as He walked 'neath Eden's mystic tree
In the cool eventide He walks with me.

I.

WHO that has seen a mountain peak,
With pines upon it, and a pure clear air
Surrounding, would not think that Christ might seek
Such place of prayer ?

II.

O purple heather ! furze of gold !
Long slopes of soft green grass, cool to the feet !
Chapels of living rock that wise men hold
For worship meet.

III.

God built them high in upper air
That those who loved Him might come close to
Him,
And you may know the wings and voices there
Of Seraphim.

IV.

Is it not beautiful to see
  Christ praying on the mountain quite alone,
From the mad whirlpool of the world set free
                To help His own ?.

V.

No soft green hill do I behold,
  No keen blue summit, kissed by sunsets rare,
But that its multitudinous mists enfold
                The Christ in prayer.

COMING OF AGE.

I.

THE poet may tread earth sadly,
    Yet is he Dreamland's king,
And the fays at his bidding gladly
    Visions of beauty bring ;
But his joys will be rarer, finer,
    Away from this earthly stage,
When he, who is now a minor,
        Comes of age.

II.

For him soft leaflets cluster
    Of violet, ivy, and vine ;
For him leaps livelier lustre
    From purple depth of wine :

Pauses the song of the Sirens,
  Closes the Sibyl's page,
Till he, whom earth environs,
    Comes of age.

III.

He is the true Anchises,
  Well Aphrodite knows,
Who has smelt her hair's sweet spices,
  And touched her bosom-snows :
Olympian food he once ate,
  This marvellous Archimage
Who, 'mid the world's great sunset,
    Comes of age.

IV.

He seems to the moiling million
  A very pestilent knave ;
Yet the sky is his pavilion,
  And the maiden moon his slave ;
And the sea, with its myriad laughter,
  And maddening freaks of rage,
Owns him who, a king hereafter,
    Comes of age.

F

V.

The wailing winds and the thunder,
  And the roar of a war that whirls,
Breaking great realms asunder,
  And the merry songs of girls,
All in one music mingle,
  All the great joys presage,
Of the poet who, royal and single,
      Comes of age.

VI.

Roll on,' O tardy cycle,
  Whose death is the poet's birth !
Blow soon, great trump of Michael,
  Shatter the crust of earth !
Let the slow spheres turn faster ;
  Hasten the heritage
Of him who, as life's true master,
      Comes of age !

BRIDAL SONG.

I.

THEY ride beneath the boughs at noon,
   A lord and lady bright,
And laugh to hear the cuckoo's tune
   And watch the swallow's flight,
And harken to the skylark's lay
   Hid in the sky's blue light. . . .
Ah, Love has laughter for the day,
   And silence for the night.

II.

The long, long day of pleasure past,
   The banquet richly dight—
The lady's eyelids droop at last
   O'er eyes of chrysolite :
The brilliant pageant fades away
   In chambers hushed and white,
Since Love has laughter for the day
   And silence for the night.

THE DAIRY MAID.

My dairy maiden, trim and tight
  Young Polly, with the merry eyes,
  I think that I can well surmise
    The meaning of their light :
For, while you skim the dainty cream,
Thro' the wide window like a dream,
You see the hay-folk bold and blithe
And one who leads, with sweeping scythe.

See now, the scythes have ceased to flash :
  The sultry toil brings sudden thirst,
  He drains the tankard who was first,
    Beneath the aerial ash.
Those stalwart shoulders look like work,
That bare brown arm will never shirk,
Those honest eyes look straight at you,
Ay, ay, my lass, the lad will do.

SCHOOL-GIRL REBELS.

A CLASS of girls, in short school robes,
Tired of Mangnall, and use of the globes,
Rebelled ; and their sage old Master said—
"Euclid or Æsop, which shall it be ?
The man who angles and circles read,
   Or the man to whom beasts and birds talked
   free ?"

The pertest girl of the rebel class,
Who doubtless grew to a charming lass,
Cried, "Æsop, certainly.   All the birds,
   And the deer that ramble the forest through,
Have pleasant music and pretty words :
   But doesn't he tell us how boys talk too ?"

A POET'S PRAYER.

HEAR, O hear!
Dionysus and Demeter!
Give, O give
Wine and bread that a poet may live!
All Olympus I disdain,
If I get the gifts of this glorious twain.

I.

RIGHT art thou, Caius Lucias Claudianus,
The men whose vile endeavours do us wrong,
The men the glories of whose triumphs pain us
May be worth money, are not worth a song.

II.

But they who rise to heights of power and splendour,
Being pure and simple, though intensely strong,
To them the poets happy homage render,
And they love song, for they are worth a song.

ON THE EVE OF A FIGHT AT SEA.

I.

I THINK that I shall die to-morrow ;
I know that, if I die, my Queen
Will for a moment feel some sorrow
'Mid joy serene.

II.

For her, for England, for my duty,
I would surrender many lives,
All thought of poesy or beauty—
A thousand wives.

III.

Some fate assures me I am going
Into a clearer, purer air :
Thank God that there will be no knowing
Of varlets there.

IV.

Sunk in the sea when fight is fervent,
No funeral will be mine, no bier :
But will my Queen for her poor servant
Drop one royal tear ?

MY OLD COAT.

I.

THIS old velvet coat has grown queer, I admit,
And changed is the colour and loose is the fit;
Though to beauty it certainly cannot aspire
'Tis a cosy old coat for a seat by the fire.

II.

When I first put it on it was awfully swell:
I went to a pic-nic, met Lucy Lepel,
Made a hole in the heart of that sweet little girl,
And disjointed the nose of her lover, the Earl.

III.

We rambled away o'er the moorland together:
My coat was bright purple, and so was the heather,
And so was the sunset that blazed in the west,
As Lucy's fair tresses were laid on my breast.

74

IV.

We plighted our troth 'neath that sunset aflame,
But Lucy returned to her Earl all the same ;
She's a grandmamma now, and is going down hill,
But my old velvet coat is a friend to me still.

V.

It was built by a tailor of mighty renown,
Whose art is no longer the talk of the town :
A magical picture my memory weaves
When I thrust my tired arms through its easy old
    sleeves.

VI.

I see in my fire, through the smoke of my pipe,
Sweet maidens of old that are long over-ripe,
And a troop of old cronies, right gay cavaliers,
Whose guineas paid well for champagne at Watier's.

VII.

A strong generation, who drank, fought, and kissed,
Whose hands never trembled, whose shots never
    missed,

Who lived a quick life, for their pulses beat high—
We remember them well, sir, my old coat and I.

VIII.

Ah, gone is the age of wild doings at Court,
Rotten boroughs, knee-breeches, hair-triggers, and
     port ;
But still I've a magnum to moisten my throat,
And I'll drink to the Past in my tattered old coat.

YOUTH.

Sweet, ah, sweet
To throw the hours away.
Tinkle, music! twinkle, feet!
Let each pulse of wild joy beat!
It is our own, this day.

No, ah, no!
Grasp we the minutes tight!
Rhyme, be silent!   Time, be slow!
Blush to rose, fair breast of snow!
It is our own, this night.

LUCIA.

Lucia! From light they named her at her birth ;
And like the light her beams were softly slender,
And like the light she gladdened all the earth,
And like the light her touch was true and
tender,
And like the light she brought both health and
mirth.
Ah, why to darkness did the stern storm send
her
Amid the deep gloom of that dread dire day ?
Since when my light of life has passed away.

" DON'T LET HIM CATCH YOU ! "

I.

On Maidenhead Thicket the moonlight of May
Throws magical beauty unknown to the day :
By the old turnpike gate where the birdcatcher
dwells
The note of a nightingale gurgles and swells.
Deep hid in the leafage of slumbering elms
She sings the sad song of the Daulian realms—
Of the web that was woven, the child that was
slain,
The flight into ether sore stricken with pain.
Though nothing the birdcatcher knows about
Greek,
He fancies that nightingale's song is unique :
And I said when the passionate music I heard—
" Don't let him catch you, beautiful bird ! "

II.

Not very far off, at the very same hour,
Two loiter together 'neath chestnuts in flower :
Faint blossoms of night give an odour divine,
Cool breath of the west is more joyous than wine.
He tells her that wondrous old story we know
(How sweet 'twas to murmur it, lustrums ago !)
And she, with the music of anguish above,
Drinks perilous draughts of the vintage of love.
Does he know, whose warm breath is so close to
　　her cheek,
More of love than the birdcatcher knows about
　　Greek ?
If not, it were time just to whisper a word :
" Don't let him catch you, beautiful bird !"

A GREEK IDYL.

I.

HE sat the quiet stream beside—
His white feet laving in the tide—
And watched the pleasant waters glide
    Beneath the skies of summer.
She singing came from mound to mound,
Her footfall on the thymy ground
Unheard; his tranquil haunt she found—
    That beautiful new comer.

II.

He said—" My own Glycerium !
The pulses of the woods are dumb,
How well I knew that thou wouldst come,
    Beneath the branches gliding."
The dreamer fancied he had heard
Her footstep, whensoever stirred
The summer wind, or languid bird
    Amid the boughs abiding.

G

III.

She dipped her fingers in the brook,
And gazed awhile with happy look
Upon the windings of a book
    Of Cyprian hymnings tender.
The ripples to the ocean raced—
The flying minutes passed in haste :
His arm was round the maiden's waist—
    That waist so very slender.

IV.

O cruel Time ! O tyrant Time !
Whose winter all the streams of rhyme,
The flowing waves of love sublime,
    In bitter passage freezes.
I only see the scambling goat,
The lotos on the waters float,
While an old shepherd with an oat
    Pipes to the autumn breezes.

MERLIN.

I.

MERLIN, the great magician,
Quelled by a woman's hand,
Lies under the mighty oak-trees
In the forest of Broceliande.

II.

The fever of life comes never
To fret his poet-brain :
He has slept a thousand years, and shall sleep
A thousand years again.

III.

Dews fall soft on the turf there,
Young birds twitter above :
Merlin sleeps, and surely sleep
Is better than aught save love.

IV.

Merlin sleeps, while the winters
　Freeze, and the summers bloom,
And the old oaks whisper softly :
　He is here till the Day of Doom.

V.

O happy, happy Merlin,
　Afar in the forest deep !
To thee alone of the sons of men
　Gave a woman the gift of sleep.

PHYLLIS.

My Phyllis is a daring rebel,
And quarrels with me, face to face,
And when she scolds she sings in treble,
And when I growl I sing in bass.

She wants the newest-fashioned kirtle ;
She wants to ask the Duke to dine.
Dear Venus, bring a rod of myrtle,
And make the pretty rascal whine.

THE TROUBADOUR'S SONG.

SWORD ! let thy temper be
  Such as shall make foes wince !
He can well use thee,
  Being a Prince.

Steed, let thy courage be
  That of thy sires long since !
He can well stride thee,
  Being a Prince.

Lady ! thy smile I see :
  Ay, and thy doom I guess,
He can well love thee.
  Be a Princess.

THE POSITIVISTS.

LIFE and the Universe show spontaneity ;
Down with ridiculous notions of Deity !
  Churches and creeds are all lost in the mists ;
  Truth must be sought with the Positivists.

Wise are their teachers beyond all comparison,
Comte, Huxley, Tyndall, Mill, Morley, and Harrison ;
  Who will adventure to enter the lists,
  With such a squadron of Positivists ?

Social arrangements are awful miscarriages ;
Cause of all crime is our system of marriages ;
  Poets with sonnets, and lovers with trysts,
  Kindle the ire of the Positivists.

Husbands and wives should be all one community,
Exquisite freedom with absolute unity ;
  Wedding rings worse are than manacled
    wrists,—
  Such is the creed of the Positivists.

There was an APE in the days that were earlier ;
Centuries passed and his hair became curlier ;
 Centuries more gave a thumb to his wrist,—
 Then he was MAN,—and a Positivist.

If you are pious (mild form of insanity),
Bow down and worship the mass of humanity.
 Other religions are buried in mists ;
 We're our own gods, say the Positivists.

SKY-MAKING.

JUST take a trifling handful, O philosopher !
Of magic matter : give it a slight toss over
   The ambient ether—and I don't see why
     You shouldn't make a sky.

O powers Utopian which we may anticipate !
Thick London fog how easy 'tis to dissipate,
   And make the most pea-soupy day as clear
     As Bass' brightest beer !

Poet-professor !   Now my brain thou kindlest !
I am become a most determined Tyndallist.
   If it is known a fellow can make skies,
     Why not make bright blue eyes ?

This to deny, the folly of a dunce it is :
Surely a girl as easy as a sunset is.
   If you can make a halo or eclipse,
     Why not two laughing lips ?

The creed of Archimedes, erst of Sicily,
And of D'Israeli . . . *forti nil difficile* . . .
   Is likewise mine.   Pygmalion was a fool
    Who should have gone to school.

Why should an author scribble rhymes or articles ?
Bring me a dozen tiny Tyndall particles ;
   Therefrom I'll coin a dinner, Nash's wine,
    And a nice girl to dine.

MATED ?

SEE her bright eyes intent upon her knights,
  While I am thinking only of my queen !
Those eyes of sapphire touch'd with fiery lights,
Like strange apocalyptic chrysolites,
        Glance o'er the mimic scene,
Where ivory warriors closely congregate,
And fight for the inevitable *Mate*.

A charming game ! Lo fingers very fair
    Touch   the   white   pawn   with   hesitation
    tremulous !
Just the least blunder in a single square
May render void the calculating care
        Of that bright bosom emulous,
And make those musical lips exclaim, " I'm fated
By you to be eternally checkmated !"

Checkmated and checkmating here to stay,
   While my sweet enemy fiercely looks or sweetly
Upon the bishops' quaint diagonal way,
Upon the castles with their solid sway,
      Would suit this child completely :
But, ah, the happiest enemies must sever,
And even a game of chess won't last for ever.

O shades of Stamma, Philidor, Carrera !
   O most miraculous Muzio, player lavish
Of peril !   Did there in your bygone era,
At your strong scientific boards, appear a
      Creature with power to ravish
Your very souls, and mingle them with hers,
Making you men as well as chess-players ?

Inexorable checkmate those eyes foresee,
   And from those soft white hands 'tis coming
     surely ;
Her sapphire eyes o'erbrim with quiet glee,
Yet look with petulant pity upon me ;
      And notice how demurely
She moves her queen—a move that's sure to tell !
She plays the game of love ten times as well.

THE WAYSIDE WELL.

I.

FULL of beauty is the wayside well,
Overcanopied with leafage pleasant,
Where the spirits of coolness love to dwell
'Mid the heat incessant.

II.

Here you see the weary wayfarer
Cool himself beneath the leafy shadow,
While the long grass scarcely seems to stir
In the unshaven meadow.

III.

Here full often rest the smoking team,
Toiling movers of the broad-wheeled waggon :
Here the vagrant artist stays to dream
O'er his pocket-flagon.

93

IV.

Hither also trips the rustic maiden
  Singing blithely through the wind-swept barley,
With her dark-red earthen pitcher laden,
    In the morning early.

V.

Talk of palm-tree shade and Arab lymph
  In the bosom of a green oasis :
Talk of water which the Naiad nymph
        'Mid dark Tempe places :

VI.

Talk of icy wine Italian quaffed
  In a cave of Pulciano's mountain :
There is nothing like a joyous draught
        From the wayside fountain.

BURNHAM BEECHES.

O, FOR a picnic here's a place,
  When the hot noon of summer kindles !
Down by express to Taplow race ;
  Refresh yourself where once was Skindle's ;
Or row from Maidenhead, if you will,
  Along the river's loveliest reaches ;
Then take the road, and drink your fill
  Of coolness 'neath the giant Beeches.

Quoth Pet to me—she's mistress now,
  I mean to be her lord and master—
" Just corrugate your manly brow,
  And prove yourself a poetaster."
Luttrel was told to do the same ;
  A lesson his example teaches ;
To an untimely end he came,
  Wanting another rhyme for " beeches."

" Pet," I replied, " some lobster first—
This fellow's the true Norway crimson ;
A goblet then to quench your thirst—
See, the bright wine the bubble swims on.
Now, would you like a slice of pine,
Or one of those voluptuous peaches,
Touch'd with a colour half divine,
Like sunset seen through Burnham Beeches?"

Ah, what a wicked witch is Pet !
Although so carefully I fed her,
And then, as far as we could get
From her mamma, I briskly led her ;
Although we criticise the trees,
And wonder what the tale of each is,
Yet she returns to—" Charlie, please,
Do write some verse on Burnham Beeches.

" Do quiz dear Amy, getting spoons
Upon that gawky little cornet ;
And Mary, with big eyes like moons,
Fainting because she saw a hornet ;

And grim old Sophonisba Snooks,
  Who tries to flirt, but only preaches
Sermons on woman's rights, and looks
  A fungus upon Burnham Beeches."

" Pet," I replied, " your rosy lips
  Were never meant for words satiric,
From graceful head to finger-tips
  Your every look's a living lyric :
I'll punish you for naughtiness."
  " O don't, dear Charlie !" she beseeches ;
Her penalty you'll have to guess :
  Secrets they keep, those grave old Beeches.

A strange magnificence of gloom
  Falls o'er the trees with falling twilight,
While hayfield's scent and lime perfume
  Delight us, driving through the shy light.
Lo, as a mighty beech we pass,
  Close at our ears a brown owl screeches,
And wicked Pet exclaims, " Alas,
  That's the true bard of Burnham Beeches !"

H

MAIDEN LADIES.

IF youth has beauty, beauty also age
Possesses, when we calmly turn the page :
A lady lovable, who love has missed,
Is like a rosebud by hot noon unkissed—
Cool shadows all her purity prolong,
And her faint fragrance lasts till evensong.

PAST AND PRESENT.

THE days of old were magic days,
    The knights so brave, the maids so fair !
Strange beauty in the forest ways,
And o'er the sea a mystic haze :
    'Twas magic everywhere.

Why these our days are magic days,
    If only we have eyes to see :
My darling has her witching ways,
Her laugh brings out the sun's bright rays,
    And fills the birds with glee.

TWO SEA SONNETS.

I.

O THOU blue Ocean ! to have been the first
  That ever tried thy wave with eager keel,
  Wondering what mystery thou wouldst reveal,
And voyaging thy solitudes, athirst
For awful sights or beautiful to burst
  Upon my longing eyes ! The first to feel
  Thy salt breath, soft as spring or sharp as steel,
And search the secrets in thy depths immerst !
Ah ! who was first ? The mighty Argonaut,
  Or the great Father of the Patriarchs three,
  For whom God bridged thee with the sevenfold
    bow ?
Would I had known thee in thy youth, and caught
  Sight of her birth who is most like to thee,
  The Lady of Love, thy daughter, long ago.

II.

I saw my Lady spring into the sea,
    And the sea loved her, and with wooing tide
    Touched her soft bosom and fair, fluttering side
And all the secrets that are sweet to me.
Next day old Ocean was awake with glee.
    Who wonders at his sudden strengthful pride,
    Having embraced my beauty and my bride
And felt her on his wild wave floating free ?
Ocean, thou art a very ancient god,
    And I have tried thee in thy happiest hour,
    And won from thee an ecstasy divine ;
Yet, though a man is moulded from a clod,
    And though a lady's only just a flower,
    Thou canst not know the glory that is mine.

THE LONELY ISLAND.

THERE is no lonelier island anywhere,
Even in silence of the southern seas,
Nor any visited by sweeter air

Than this, whereon do stand the three great trees;
Old giants, in whose boughs there dwells always
The baffled buried murmur of a breeze.

There two bright children, through long summer
    days,
Make a fair world, build hourly halls of wonder
From water and air, soft light and silver haze,

Arch of the rainbow, sable belt of thunder,
All that dear Mother Nature offers those
Whom fate from home's delight has torn asunder.

And if their solitary pleasure knows
Some interruption, it is just the touch
That, like a dream, makes perfect our repose.

For no one should be happy overmuch,
And no one should deem happiness the thing
Above all others for the hand to clutch.

KATE TEMPLE'S SONG.

I.

ONLY a touch, and nothing more :
Ah ! but never so touched before !
Touch of lip, was it ?   Touch of hand ?
Either is easy to understand.
Earth may be smitten with fire or frost—
Never the touch of true love lost.

II.

Only a word, was it ?   Scarce a word !
Musical whisper, softly heard,
Syllabled nothing—just a breath—
'Twill outlast life, and 'twill laugh at death.
Love with so little can do so much—
Only a word, sweet !   Only a touch !

VENUS ASLEEP.

On this green path, through this deep glade,
Lovers may linger, unafraid
  Of the unloving world, whose way
          Is to betray.

Through fluttering leaves the dim lights gleam
Leading, misleading, like a dream :
  Each turn o' the path has marvels new—
          That's Love's way too.

Lo, now a cavern, dark and cool,
Green moss beside a shadowy pool,
  Such silence as the hush'd air keeps
          When Venus sleeps.

O loitering lover, be thou wise—
Kiss softly lips, kiss gently eyes,
  Lest the delicious spell thou break,
          And Venus wake.

A LITTLE LECTURE.

I.

SIT still, child, if you know the way,
 Cross your white arms upon your breast ;
Let the dark glory of your hair
 From bands escape.
'Tis weary always to be gay ;
 And sweet is silence, sweet is rest :
We drink the juices of despair
 From Life's crushed grape.

II.

Why should I lecture ?   You are young,
 And tameless as a dragon-fly,
And beautiful to look upon,
 And sweet to touch.

106

Nothing you know of nerves unstrung,
Nor can believe that you will die,
And go where other girls have gone.
I ask too much.

III.

Pshaw! Flutter like a pretty bird,
Outrun the wind, outlaugh the brooks,
Flout the frail ferns with flying feet,
Outblush the rose ;
Let your young petulant voice be heard
Joyous through all the forest-nooks.
But have you got a soul, my sweet ?
Who knows ? Who knows ?

GOLDEN DAYS.

O GOLDEN days that I have known
  Amid the roses, happy child !
With fragrance through the foliage blown,
And dreams that came to me alone,
And merry music always new
From gay birds singing, as they flew,
  Wayward notes and wild !

O golden days 'tis mine to know
  When Love's sweet lesson I shall learn !
No fragrance of the rarest flowers,
No visions of the laziest hours,
No music of a myriad birds,
No melody of poet's words,
  Tells all for which I yearn.

108

A VILLAGE SONG.

JUST in her teens,
With eyelids drooped demure,
And gravity that could not long endure,
The child sat knitting by the well,
Her careless bosom rose and fell :
It was the prettiest of country scenes.

Her laugh broke out
A kitten among girls,
A merry creature glad to toss her curls
But forced to knit, nor ever stir,
By a most pious grandmother.
What is that pious grandmother about ?

WINDS AND WOMEN.

''. . . mulier cupido quod dicit amanti
In vento et rapidâ scribere oportet aqua.''
CATULLUS.

THE South wind blew, and its breath was a song,
As we loiter'd the shore along
Under the light of the sun-kiss'd moon,
Setting soon.
Whisper'd the ripples, murmur'd the leaves,
Melody soft of the autumn eves ;
But the song of the South came sweeter far,
Like a voice from Venus, evening star.

And I said, " O women and winds, they change,
And through every point of the compass range !
Who cares for the daughter of Aquilo,
Fast yet slow ?

With the eagle's scream and the eagle's beak,
That's the woman of science, a creature unique."
My lady laugh'd, and her rosy mouth
Seem'd to echo the song of the South.

" Daughter of Eurus is still worse churl,
With her stinging sneer at a prettier girl,
With scandalous stories eager to blight
                    Love's delight.
Never she'll tread Cythera's glade,
But go to the devil a sour old maid."
Like the drip of a fountain crystal clear
Was my lady's laugh at the words severe.

" But the musical daughter of Auster sings
Melody sweeter than aught with wings ;
And thy nymph as a wooer comes to us,
                    Zephyrus !
The girl of the South is a fairy flower,
With a fragrance strange at the midnight hour ;
The girl of the West is a deep red rose,
On whose happy breast there is sweet repose."

The moon was dipping.   My lady laugh'd :
" Little you know of a woman's craft.
I, to a bore or a canting priest,
                              Blow due East ;
I've a Northern chill for the fools who annoy,
And a Southern song for lovers of joy ;
And now I shift to the West, and woo
Somebody—somebody : you know who."

WHO IS KING?

STREPSIADES. See what a fine thing education is ! My
Pheidippides, there is no Zeus.
PHEIDIPPIDES. Well, who is there then ?
STREPSIADES. Whirl is King, having turned out Zeus.
ARISTOPHANES, *Clouds*.

Is there anything new beneath
The sun ?   Upon land or sea
    Or in air where meteors swing. . . .
In city or desolate heath
Can there verily be
    One new thing ?

Why the absolute Attic wit
Heard by Ilissus the fools
    Hideously maundering . . .

I   113

Zeus they declined to permit
Place in their learned schools :
    Whirl was King !

So the Professors by Thames
Having disestablished God
    Hold it an excellent thing :
For lo ! there is none who condemns
The dull sons of the sod :
    Fog is King.

And poetry flies afar
From the city where Shakespeare made
    Air with his music ring :
Idiots and harlots are
Chiefs of the mimic trade :
    Dirt is King.

And they who stand in the place
Of the hero-statesmen who once
    Could glory to England bring,
Dread the enemy's face,
Of a type half-coward half-dunce :
    Fear is King.

Not always shall it be so,
Though dominant fools and knaves
  To their evil eminence cling :
In their heart of hearts men know,
However the sciolist raves—
  God is King.

KING ATOM.

" Atom is King again "— King indestructible ;[1]
Tyndall recrowns him, a fate ineluctable :
    Hear his oration of vehemence vast
    Made to the Monarch enthroned at Belfast.

" Hymn the great Autocrat now in no puny verse !
Did he not build the material universe ?
    Atom to atom by tendency flies,
    Making all forms 'twixt the seas and the
    skies.

" Atom is God, as is clear to the curious ;
Every other divinity spurious.
    Atom wrote *Hamlet*, 'tis easy to see :
    Who wrote the Bible is nothing to me."

[1] Æneis, viii. 334.

Really, O Tyndall, 'tis hardly facetious,
Crambe recocta of hapless Lucretius.
  Surely to God you could never be blind
  If you had only an atom of mind.

Farseeing physicist, does it occur to you
(Question I put without meaning a slur to you)
  That, knowing much that you brilliantly teach,
  Others can see what your eye cannot reach?

'Tis so in physics, why not in ontology?
If you would think, we should get an apology,
  Sounding the universe, travelling so far,
  Can you be sure 'tis the uttermost star?

For an inspired and ideal delightedness
Are we to have scientific shortsightedness?
  Strengthen your telescope, Tyndall the blind!
  You see King Atom, but God is behind.

A GAME OF CHESS.

I.

TERRACE and lawn are white with frost,
   Whose fretwork flowers upon the panes—
A mocking dream of summer, lost
      'Mid winter's icy chains.

II.

White-hot, indoors, the great logs gleam,
   Veiled by a flickering flame of blue :
I see my love as in a dream—
      Her eyes are azure, too.

III.

She puts her hair behind her ears
   (Each little ear so like a shell),
Touches her ivory Queen, and fears
      She is not playing well.

IV.

For me, I think of nothing less :
I think how those pure pearls become her—
And which is sweetest, winter chess
      Or garden strolls in summer.

V.

O linger, frost, upon the pane !
O faint blue flame, still softly rise !
O, dear one, thus with me remain,
      That I may watch thine eyes !

BOY AND GIRL.

Two fishers went where the river is bright,
  And one was a girl and one was a boy ;
And one caught just a day's delight,
And the other caught grief for murk midnight ;
  O 'tis a world of sorrow and joy !

Two travellers soared in an air-balloon,
  And one was a boy and one was girl,
And one fell down from the car too soon,
And the other was scorched in the sun's hot
    noon !
  O 'tis a world of wonder and whirl !

ANTIQUITY.

THE eagle said, " I am old ; "
Said the tomtit, " I'm older than you "—
A ball of green and gold,
   That had counted summers two.

And the jackdaw said, from his perch,
   A pulpit of gray old stone,
" 'Twas I first founded the Church :
Leave questions of age alone."

And the raven came with a croak,
   A mixture of humour and woe,
And claimed the Druid's oak
   And the magical mistletoe.

But the eagle, far withdrawn,
   Remembered old royal words,
When on Eden's sun-touched lawn
   GOD said, " Let us make the birds."

And away into ether rare,
And close to the sun's fierce gold,
Rose the king of the kings of the air,
Crying, " Ay, I am young ! I am old."

A LEAFLET.

O WONDERFUL wild world of ours !
  O spring's soft breath !
O coming kisses ; coming flowers—
  And coming death !

The flower's a fruit, the kiss a boy,
  The maid a wife—
And sorrow is the root of joy,
  And death is life.

APRIL FOOLS.

COMES April, her white fingers wet with flowers,
And we might well enjoy her sunny showers,
If the malignant Fate which o'er us rules
  Did not bring April Fools.

Fools who will whisper, you and I together
Ought not to wander in the sweet spring weather,
For I'm a boy and you're a girl, and so
  'Tis very wrong, you know.

To hunt for violets in meadows fair
Till April rains her diamonds on your hair,
Is really such a silly girlish fashion,
  It puts them in a passion.

Youth's joy must have its grim concomitants,
Its sulky sisters and its maiden aunts.
Well, let them scowl at us, and keep their rules—
  We won't be April Fools.

ISIS.

O ISIS ! gentle Isis ! flowing on
   Through meadows green with odorous delight,
   Through woods that rustle with the breezy flight
Of wondrous dwellers in the deep unknown ;
Soft is thy music, and in unison
   With the star-whispers of the eloquent night ;
   Glad are thy waters in the golden light
Dropt from the long locks of Hyperion.

O Isis ! noble Isis ! in thee quivers
   Eternal Oxford's wondrous Gothic glory,
   Poetic towers and pinnacles of pride :
And, loftier in thy power than classic rivers,
   Changing thy name by some green promontory,
   Thou lavest London with an ampler tide.

MARTIAL IN LONDON.

EXQUISITE wines and comestibles,
From Slater, and Fortnum and Mason ;
Billiards, *écarté*, and chess-tables ;
Water in vast marble basin ;
Luminous books (not voluminous)
To read under beech-trees cacuminous ;
One friend who is fond of a distich,
And doesn't get too syllogistic ;
A valet, who knows the complete art
Of service ;—a maiden, his sweetheart ;
Give me these, in some rural pavilion,
And I'll envy no Rothschild his million.

TO MY MUSE IN NOVEMBER.

Fuit! The lingering year's last leaf has fled
  Down a fog-laden wind with doleful flutter,
It lately crown'd my plane-tree's towering head ;
  It lies—with an old shoe—in yonder gutter.
Sharer of sunny hours and summer sweets,
  Dear Muse, thy fire dies down to its last ember ;
What inspiration haunts the sodden streets
          Of dull November ?

Fuit! Great Phœbus fails ; his fieriest lance
  Falls blunt before Fog's buckler. Valorous
      Cupid
Arms against Dulness, but *his* arrows glance.
  The sad, the slow, the solemn, and the stupid
Have now their hour. Death-pale is passion's rose ;
  Wit is as faint of flight as humdrum duty,
And Beauty with a smut upon her nose
          Is scarcely Beauty.

127

Dear Muse, we are foredone.   These clinging
    clouds
And carboniferous vapours damp and dull us.
I'm sure such sooty suffocating shrouds
    Had choked the songs of Ovid or Tibullus.
Asphyxia warbles no Horatian stanza,
    Dulcetly gay or daintily satiric ;
As well might Sycorax or Sancho Panza
            Ape Ariel's lyric.

O, for the lands where burning Sappho breathed,
    And Sangster's silk umbrellas were no part
Of the bard's outfit ; where rose-incense wreathed—
    Not clouds of fog—the shrines of love and art !
The dithyrambic fervour must die out
    In limbo-lands, far north of Wit's equator,
Where the Muse dares not go about without
            Her respirator.

O month of mist, miasma, murky skies,
    Fogs, fires, and civic feeds, our dismal city
Is thy chief thrall !   Could Socrates be wise,
    Anacreon gaily amorous, Lucian witty,

Beneath thy spell ? The demon Dulness rules
   In torpor god-defying, dunce-delighting,
And 'gainst the joint array of fogs and fools
          What use in fighting ?

.   .   .   .   .

And yet the memory of Muriel's face
   Amidst the roses in that far-off garden,
Even to glum November lends such grace
   As might have gleam'd from leafy June in Arden.
You have no fog *là-bas*, love ; silvery mist
   Is all that ever hides your hills and hollows ;
But I believe those eyes of amethyst
          Would beat Apollo's,

And pierce this Stygian gloom. I'm very sure
   Dulness would die before your arrowy laughter.
The "blacks" would spare that beauty pale and
   pure—
"You solemn scribe, whatever are you after ? "
Herself ! A rosebud at her breast ! My Muse
   Incarnate, bright in every mould and member !
Vale ! I've no more time for dull abuse
          Of dull November.

K

A TRIFLE.

THEY loved and laughed, they kissed and chaffed,
  They threw the happy hours away :
That's the way the world goes round—
  That's the story of Yesterday.

They talk of fate and calculate,
  And keep accounts, and measure, and weigh :
That's the way the world goes round—
  That's the story of To-day.

They'll see on high in yonder sky
  The God whose power destroyeth sorrow :
That's the way the world goes round—
  That's the story of To-morrow.

A GIRL—A HORSE—A TREE.

I.

A GIRL, a Horse, a Tree—
No more—and yet to me
  A picture unforgotten evermore ;
Burnt suddenly into this brain of mine
As sunlight stamps on vaporous iodine
  The far wild restless sea, the silent shore.

II.

By the blue winding Trent
That elm magnificent
  Spread heavy branches through the summer air ;
Fast fluttering shadows of its foliage fell
Upon a fairy form I knew too well,
  Haughtily sitting her brown Arab mare.

III.

I spoke—I know not why.
Was it the summer sky,
The Trent's delicious reach of azure light,
The mellow cadences of amorous birds,
Opening the fount of foolish loving words?
Who knows?   She passed for ever from my sight.

IV.

Ah, her brown startled eyes—
Her haughty lip's surprise—
Her tremulous little hand—her fluttered breast!
That picture strangely bitter, strangely sweet,
By the great river in the summer heat,
Must dwell upon my brain, till death brings rest.

CAMPKIN ! dear friend, your Martial is divine,
And strong the music of your sounding line :
Marcus Valerius Martialis might
Thank you himself for judging him aright,
E'en tho' within his fields of epigram
You wander not.   Yet very sure I am,
If you had pass'd the heavy Latin gates,
Too often open'd for mere addlepates,
You would have been at home, and felt the fire
Of the great masters of the Roman lyre.
You might have been more learned, I surmise,
But not more friendly, Campkin; not more wise,
Nor could you say to friend a pleasant thing
In silver verse of more sonorous ring.
Thanks for your Martial : 'tis of books a flower,
And I shall waste on it full many an hour.
Oak fitly binds such book, I hold it true ;
For English heart of oak I come to you.

UNDER THE CLIFFS.

I.

WHITE-THROATED Maiden, gay be thy carol
Under the cliffs by the sea ;
Plays the soft wind with thy dainty apparel—
Ah, but thou think'st not of me.
Stately and slow
The great ships go,
White gulls in the blue float free ;
And my own dear May
Sees the skies turn gray
Under the cliffs by the sea.

II.

Ah, there is one who follows thee lonely
Under the cliffs by the sea :
Joy to this heart if thy watchet eyes only
Turn for a moment on me.

Strange is thy gaze
O'er the ocean's haze,
With those white hands claspt on thy knee:
Sweet breast, flutter high
For a true-love nigh
Under the cliffs by the sea!

III.

When shall I dare love's story to utter
Under the, cliffs by the sea?
When shall I feel thy little heart flutter,
Press'd, O my darling, to me?
Lo, the foam grows dark,
And the white-winged barque
Seems a speck in the mist to be:
Ere the sun's rim dips
Let me kiss those lips
Under the cliffs by the sea!

OCTOBER.

O THE misty bright October!
  Misty-bright on the brown hillside—
Setters hunt the stubble over,
Scream the crake and the golden plover
  Through the moorland waste and wide.

O the golden-crowned October!
  Golden, gorgeous in decay:
Through the woods the leaves for ever
Drift, and in the sluggish river
  Yellow and brown they drift away.

O the chill and pale October!
  Colder winds are whirling now—
All the champaign wide they deaden,
Will not suffer the leaves to redden,
  Hanging lone on the wintry bough.

O the merry and glad October !
Heap the hearth with lots of fuel :
Blaze away both log and splinter ;
Hail to the coming of healthful winter—
Hail to the festive joys of Yule !

LILYLEAF.

A PERFECT little beauty, warm and white,
With eyes the colour of cool chrysolite
Beneath soft eyelids tremulous.   In brief,
　　　　　I call her Lilyleaf.

There hovers over her the strange intense
Perfume of pleasure that transcends the sense,
Commingling pain and rapture, glory and grief:
　　　　　Such is my Lilyleaf.

Her commonest word is melody complete,
Her gayest kiss is passion, honey-sweet,
But loving, loving, loving is the chief
　　　　　Beauty of Lilyleaf.

ON THE MOORS.

WE'VE removed the political blister ;
And Wyndham, whose wife and whose sister
   Are charming, has taken a moor :
He writes, " You must rough it, old fellow ;
This box with old age has grown mellow,
   But I hope you won't think it a bore."

A bore ! In the first place, there's Wyndham—
There are no jolly sins but he's sinn'd 'em ;
   He's always in love or in debt.
Than his wife there's no beauty that's blonder ;
But perchance of gay Jessy I'm fonder—
   A mischievous merry brunette.

That shooting-box, worse for the weather
Of years, nested snug amid heather,
   With a beck tripping noisily by,—

I have known it three capital seasons,
And have given three excellent reasons
    Why thither from London I fly.

But if Wyndham, his lady, and Jessy,
Wild-witty and daintily-dressy,
    Suffice not your critical nous,
This reason, O friend and O brother,
I give you, a fourth, yea another—
    That moor has abundance of grouse.

O, joyous the luncheon at noon is,
When languor conducive to spoon is !
    The ladies on ponies come up,
And bring us cold birds and flirtation—
Combined, a delightful sensation,
    With really miraculous cup.

Then at night the half-dinner, half-supper ;
And Jessy sings songs (out of Tupper,
    It may be, or possibly mine),
And cavendish lends its aroma ;
And laziness, lotos, and coma
    Make the heart of the Highlands divine.

Dear Editor, he is the true sage
Who of happy occasions makes usage,
    Selecting Time's loveliest gems :
Perhaps I'm as snug in the Highlands
As you where the willow-crown'd islands
    Break full-flowing current of Thames.

THE MINOR CANON.

ME, living in an old cathedral close,
A minor canon, quietude befits,
And theologic philosophic thought.
Tranquil my days and solitary : only
When Gerald comes, my joyous artist-brother,
To shock me with his fancies.   Fresh he comes
From sketching in the core of Wales or Devon,
From strife to find out how to paint the sea
By plunging sheer into the unresting tide,
From all the Quixote-like Bohemian life
Which painters know.   He from my folios wakes
Me, dreaming over ancient subtleties
Which never have been solved and never will.
And " Pshaw, my boy," he says, as at dessert
Over our claret (for he rails at port
As wine ecclesiastic) and some peaches
Wasp-bitten, and a yellow-rinded melon,

Produce of my quaint garden-quadrangle,
We sit conversing, " Pshaw," quoth Gerald, " you—
Why what a most ridiculous life you lead !
Look at the daughters of your friend the Dean
Tripping across the close.   Three days a week
You see them, yet you never fall in love.
If I were here a fortnight, I should be
In love with both.   How picturesque they look
'Neath the great oak trees at the Deanery
Working, or playing chess, or reading *Maud*,
Or anything you like !   In Amy's eyes
The unsuspected love comes twinkling up
Like bubbles in a goblet of Champagne."

To whom I answer slowly, " Pretty, yes.
But why should I rub off the sweet girl-bloom ?
No, let me dwell with my theology."
" And what do you know of theology ?
Here, in the great Apocalypse, which ends
The holy gladness of the Testament,
As some loud-voiced strong-lightninged thunder-
    storm
Ends a calm summer, I perceive that days
Will come when heaven and earth shall pass away

And other heavens o'erarch a fairer earth,
And ocean shall not wash the shores of earth,
Why 'no more sea,' my brother?"

" Why indeed,
Except that ocean typifies the rite
Of baptism, which with sin shall pass away—
Except that ocean typifies unrest,
And we shall rest for ever?"

"Reasons strange,"
Gerald incredulous replies.   " Must men
Never again in that new world look forth
Upon the wild blue sea, to suit your types?
How many a weary traveller, soiled with dust,
After long miles beneath a pitiless sun
On white monotonous roads, catches a glimpse
Of the remote blue ocean all alive
With yachts and trawlers—a great warship perhaps
Spreading white canvas to the wooing south—
And thinks, *Ah surely on the sea is rest!*
Toil on the mainland, rest upon the main!
Nay, brother mine, explain in other fashion.
Earth without ocean were like some fair face

In whose too-lustrous eyes no crystal tear
Had ever glistened."

Then he gulps his claret
And leaves me hastily.   Perchance I dream,
Some twenty minutes after, looking out
Where moonlight chequers the cathedral close
With shivering shadows of the mighty trees,
That he and Amy, he and little Amy,
Sweet brown-eyed daughter of my friend the Dean,
Stroll up and down beneath the immortal towers,
And talk in music, as a brooklet talks
To its beloved woodlands all night long.

DEVOTION.

AT church she looked on me a minute,
  Then turned to read the holy book.
Methinks : well now, the devil's in it . . .
  If she hated me, she wouldn't look.

She looks but little at the parson :
  She looks still less upon the clerk ;
But when she looks at me 'tis arson—
  Her eyes send forth so fierce a spark.

I waited for her after matins,
  Where the old ivy's grown a tree.
Perhaps I slightly crushed her satins.
  The ivy trembled : so did she.

AN APRIL LETTER.

HAVE the snow-storms taken flight ?
Are there heaps of violets white ?
Do the children's fingers go
Into that soft fragrant snow ?
'Tis the sweetest time o' the year :
Soon the swallows will be here :
Swims the swift across the foam ;
Sings the thrush at evenglome.
  So, as all the world is gay,
  Let's be April fools to-day.

Long ere you were robed in silk
I was sent for pigeon's milk :
Gravely now this planet rolls ;
Bills I keep in pigeon-holes.
Still I love the twilight hush,
And the self-repeating thrush,

147

And a lady's fancies fair,
Suited to the sweet spring air.
　　So, till care the spirit cools,
　　Let us both be April fools.

I forget : you play at whist,
So your wisdom would be missed.
Whist's to me an awful joke—
You should see how I revoke.
Knaves and aces I detest—
Kings are duller than the rest ;
Only card that joy imparts
Is my lady Queen of Hearts.
　　Throw the ace of trumps away !
　　Let's be April fools to-day.

SPRING.

O FRESH flower-litany of spring !
     Each year it comes with sweet surprise :
No deeper blue the violet knew,
No sunnier was the crocus-gold,
No greener tinge had snowdrop fringe,
       Than when in times grown old
       They greeted childish eyes.

O bright bird-litany of Spring !
     The robin sang the winter thro',
But now the lark is up i' the dark,
Brown mavis carols o'er lawn and glen,
With golden bill the black merles trill,
       Flutters the atom wren,
       The birds are wild to woo.

Fresh flowers that spring ! Bright birds that sing !
    Alien and yet akin are we.
By rill and stream of care men dream,
And nought can cure their fever-fret :
But no trouble have I 'twixt turf and sky
       When laughs my darling pet
       With birds and flowers and me.

OLDER.

I.

OLDER, but not half so wise :
Now we have a sense of shame ;
Once we played—boy and maid—
Void of thought, a happy game.

II.

Older, but not half so wise :
Now we have a sense of gold.
Long ago gold might go . . .
Coin might wait till souls grew old.

III.

Older, but not half so wise :
Now we have a sense of sin.
Children fair may not dare
Love and laugh and woo and win.

LOVE-STRIFE.

I.

I WONDER whether I love her;
I wonder whether I hate.
Now she will coo like a milk-white dove,
   All love;
 Now she stands like a queen apart,
 Crowned with beauty: but, has she a heart?
  O could I only discover
    Whether I love or hate,
    Then should I know my fate.

II.

I wonder if for a minute
 She thinks of me when away;
If she deems me a trivial toy,
   Mere boy:

Yes, I can fancy, yes, I can see
Rosy red lips that laugh at me.
   O love's strife ! I'll begin it :
      Throwing all fear away,
      I'll know my fate this day.

HOME.

WE will not live in Italy or Greece,
   My bride, my beautiful. Though skies are blue,
   And the air odorous, and our spirits renew
Great visions there which have been made to cease
By the Destroyer, yet the gay caprice
   Of Fancy alone those visions could indue
   With happiness. O, all the long years through,
England for us ! A little realm of peace
By the most joyous of its haunted meres
   And rivers of romance. Together there
   We will grow old in pious humbleness :
And if our chalice must be filled with tears,
   Be Love our cupbearer ; and no despair
   Or agony shall our twin hearts possess.

THE VILLAGE GREEN.

THE fiddler plays in the summer eve,
　While the lads dance, and the lasses too :
Who would care to mope or grieve
　When the lark sings in the summer blue ?

The music flies to the sapphire skies,
　To the lads' heels, to the lasses' breast.
Dance, dance, while the sunset dies
　Purple and amber, deep in the West.

QUEEN AND SLAVE.

I.

O HAPPY life, whose love is found !
O happy love, whose life is free !
O happy strings whose soft notes sound
Athwart the sea !

II.

The sea has mistress in the moon,
The moon has lover in the sea,—
They meet too late, they part too soon—
And so do we.

III.

I am adored, yet must obey ;
I am a queen and yet a slave.
It seems to me the self-same way
With moon and wave.

IV.

O be it so ! O let it be !
O may I always rule and serve,
And live the life whose love is free,
And never swerve !

BLONDE AND BRUNETTE.

THERE'S a beautiful blonde for whom
I have been mad in my time full oft :
O, her kiss hath a gay perfume !
O, her voice is divinely soft !
Sweet it is her waist to clasp,
Strongly she mankind can grasp ;
While life lasts I shall ever be fond
Of that same peerless piquant blonde.

There is also a rare brunette,
Years ago beloved by me ;
Purple suns that in autumn set
Have not more magical hue than she.
O, to woo her is joy and power !
She, of brunettes the choicest flower,
Hath a deliciously dainty breath :
Faith, I shall love her until my death.

For the laughing blonde is Champagne, you see :
And the rare brunette is Burgundy.

158

CRYING WOLF.

A SHEPHERD boy on the hillside high,
  Lazy, mischievous, fond of fun,
  Glad to get home ere day was done,
    Cried *Wolf!*
    Cried *Wolf!*
Till the Wolf came, and 'twas vain to cry.

A gay young fellow with giddy head,
  Always caught by a pretty face,
  Flirted with all the female race. . . .
    Sang *I love!*
    Sang *I love!*
Till he sang to a widow, who made him wed.

LIFE.

THEY say the world is very sad
  From the sun's hot noon to the round full
  moon :
While there's in it a lass and a lad
  Sorrow's a thing will perish soon.

I say the world is a world of joy,
  With the sweet birds' tune in the summer
  swoon.
Make not of life a broken toy—
  Beauty's a thing will perish soon.

CAUSIDICUS AD CANEM.

My old Dog stands by the Temple Stairs,
 Watching the water's turbid flow,
And he thinks, as the Autumn sunlight glares,
 This is a river he ought to know.

He gives a strange suspicious sniff
 As he sees the dark stream eddy along,
And dreams of a lazy loitering skiff,
 Of a Lover's laugh, of a Lady's song.

First drops of a deluge, heavy and warm,
 Under Marlow Bridge had driven us three,
And we rocked in our boat in the thunderstorm :
 If either grew tired, dear Dog, 'twas he.

Ah, the days are here for the straining oars—
 The life and the love our toil to crown !
You shall splash, old boy, from the soft green
  shores
 Of a river unsoiled by London town.

M

SERENADE.

GOOD-NIGHT! The world is still :
No echo from the hill :
Without a sound the stars pass through the silent
sky.
The sweet leaves are not stirred
By chirp of wakeful bird,
Or by late lover's word :
Amid a drowsy world alone awake am I.
Ah, lady, sleeping sound,
While the great world goes round !
To be a vision of yours I would be glad to die.
Good-night ! Good-bye !

SUNSET.

HELEN and I looked out upon the west.
O unimaginable sunset !   O
Soft sky in mystic waves of colours drest,
With great Apollo's final kiss aglow !
O lights that lessen, linger, glisten, grow !
Almighty Artist, never do I see
Thy little lightest touch of fire or snow.
Of bird that sings, of blossom upon tree,
Without that inner silent saying : *I love Thee.*

MIDNIGHT IS MINE.

Μεσονυκτίοις ποθ' ὥραις,
Στρέφεται ὅτ' Ἄρκτος ἤδη
Κατὰ χεῖρα τὴν Βοώτου.

ANACREON.

LET the hot noon with all its pomp and splendour
   Revel in sunlight rich as golden wine,
Making the lover strong, the lady tender,
   Filling the wide green glades with dreams divine,
Bringing a calm to which we all surrender
   Like halcyon brooding on the hyaline :
      Yet Midnight's mine.

Midnight ! the stars' most marvellous procession ;
   Strong planets that above the horizon shine ;
The gliding moon, that in sweet silent session,
   Looks on a world that worships at her shrine—
For lunacy is surely earth's possession,
   Blood being shed for naught by Seine and Rhine :
      Yes, Midnight's mine.

Is it for work? There comes no fool to bore us :
Midnight intoxicates the human swine.
Ay, they are uttering now the snore sonorous—
Such folk drink heavily whene'er they dine.
I, pen in hand, with all the gods for chorus,
Write then my clearest thought, my noblest line.
Midnight is mine.

Is it for joy? The lamps are burning gaily,
The pretty dancers pass with footstep fine,
Now is the time some lady sweet to waylay,
And flirt o'er foaming fluid festucine :
Such pastime nightly drowns the dose we daily
Get of the canter's rot, the patriot's whine.
Midnight is mine.

Is it for love? Ah, happy hours, too holy
For deftest chronicle in daintiest line !
Apart, alone, entranced by passion wholly,
We taste the sweetness that will make no sign.
Dear Lady of Dreams, thy silver chariot slowly
Will cross the aërial arch toward sunrise-shine.
Midnight is mine.

COUPLETS.

IMPERFECT utterance is our saddest taint,
And, when our hearts grow full, our lips grow faint.

WHAT we call life is twilight : when 'tis done,
A door is opened, and we see the sun.

JOY is time's pander, Pleasure is time's thief,
But time's two conquerors are Toil and Grief.

TO F. C.

1ST APRIL 1876.

Now if to be an April Fool
    Is to delight in the song of the thrush,
To long for the swallow in air's blue hollow,
    And the nightingale's riotous music-gush,
And to paint a vision of cities Elysian
    Out away in the sunset-flush—
Then I grasp my flagon and swear thereby,
We are April Fools, my Love and I.

And if to be an April Fool
    Is to feel contempt for iron and gold,
For the shallow fame at which most men aim—
    And to turn from worldlings cruel and cold
To God in His splendour, loving and tender,
    And to bask in His presence manifold—
Then by all the stars in His infinite sky,
We are April Fools, my Love and I.

A MAY LYRIC.

I.

THE robin's nest in our dark yew
  Is safe to-night.   I see
Brown hen asleep on her snug nest,
And saucy cock with crimson breast,
  Above upon the tree.

II.

Ah ! happy birds, whose love is true,
  Enjoy the murmurous May !
Be mine, like yours, the real delight
Of sleeping by my love all night,
  Of singing half the day !

FRAGMENTS OF THE COMEDY OF
DREAMS.

Astrologos. Strong races run to goodness or to
wickedness.
The nation that gave Christ gave too Iscariot ;
Isaiah's kinsman cries " Old Clo !" beneath me
here ;
I wonder what your fate will be, Prince Raphael,
Whose father strongest was of men, and wickedest,
Whose father's father was a King of Chivalry ?
Raphael. Nay, wonder not, old friend : the
problem's soluble ;
I have the perfect power of loving loveliness.

———————

Raphael. I am adventurous, who would fain be
indolent.
Astrologos. Venus and Mars conjunct at your
nativity

Gave love of luxury, with power of princeliness ;
With you, my lord, 'tis always fight or festival.

Astrologos. If London be the world's most noble
 city, then
Who dwells therein should be no common citizen,
The world's most noble title, greater far than all
Dukes, but not *duces*, Earls not free from churlish-
 ness,
Should be the sounding civic name of Londoner.
 Raphael. Lofty ideal ! But the race of cockneys
 are
As commonplace a set as you'll see anywhere ;
A race that loves the billiard-room and music-hall,
And tripe and onions, and hot spirits afterward.
 Astrologos. Wait, Count, until you meet a
 perfect Londoner,
A man who knows that City's penetralia,
Master of fashion, politics, and gaiety,
Swimmer on summit wave of choice society.
A Londoner, my lord, is not *faex Londini ;*
He lives in Clubland, gossips at the Travellers',

Checkmates a Bishop at the Athenæum ; and
Loiters away to play whist at the Arlington.
Dining alone, his dinner is a work of art ;
And, dining out, his wit turns meal to festival.
Always himself, cool, easy, careless, nonchalant,
Whether he helps a fair Princess to strawberries
(Bright eyes may languish under royal eyelashes)
Or heads a merry crew to Richmond, wondering
Which they like best, the Heidseck or the nightin-
    gales.
    Alouette. Papa, I should so like to know a
    Londoner.

    Astrologos. There is a tide in the affairs of man,
    my Prince,
Which, taken at the flood, may lead——
    Raphael.   To Jericho !
Why do you murder the immortal Englishman ?
Hear this : there is a moment when a woman's
    heart
Beats to the tune of love, but beats inaudibly
To the poor fools not meant to win and marry her.

Alas, the life that once we lived has fled away ;
Lost, lost, beyond the hope of a recovery.
Love's blushing flowers have faded very long ago ;
And if there was a creature strangely beautiful,
Who caught your heart within her hand and
    crushed it there
Till the blood left it—who could fool and flatter
    you
In the sweet summer, under leaf-tent tremulous,
With ripe rose-mouth that your sun-kiss made
    rosier,
And then who did . . . what's nameless . . . call
    her Perdita.

—————

O the gay school life !   The impartial Common-
    wealth !
Homage to finest classic, finest cricketer :
Homage to master of the sculls or algebra.
Who would not gladly be a reckless boy again ?
School is a kingdom where no sneak we tolerate :
School is a country where to lie is kickable :
A rare oasis in that desert, memory.

—————

Astrologos. Strange sights men see who do
strange deeds unscrupulous.

Raphael. I have done stranger wilder deeds
than any man,
Yet, save that rascals fawned on me that hated me,
And ladies loved me much that should have hated
me,
I have seen no sight strange enough to talk about.

Astrologos. Wait.

────────

Astrologos. He has come back again, you see.
I knew he would.
One of these nights the drowsy-eyed astronomer,
Watching the stars in an enormous speculum,
Will start to see the missing Pleiad back again.

────────

Astrologos. I have known men who died, and
came to life again ;
I have known men who died, and came to death
again.
I have known men who neither lived nor died at
all,

But were pure phantoms, shadows on the atmos-
phere.
Raphael. Poor ghosts, who shivered through the
world.

Alouette. Papa, Prince Raphael tells me I am
beautiful.
Astrologos. Stand up, you little chit, and let
me look at you.
Well, yes, your figure's lithe, curves not too
prominent,
Your eyes sea-water colour, when a breeze is out,
Your shoulders are not villainously angular,
Your waist is not too narrow.
             Walk ! Ah, excellent :
A woman's walk is perfect test of ladyhood.
But . . . Princes surely should not call you
beautiful.

Alouette. They say, papa, princes sometimes
are scandalous . . .
Do wickedness, say wickedness.

Astrologos.   Believe it not ;
Those are the dreams of your untutored babyhood.
Princes are like the stars, which move in rhythmical
Curves of the infinite cone, above all questionings.
    Alouette. And yet *you* ask your questions of the
    Pleiades,
The Hyades, Arcturus, Rigel, Sirius.
What is the use ?
    Astrologos.   Be off to bed, Miss Prateapace.

Astrologos. The petty parallelograms of life
Spoil it : the terrible right angle tyrannises.
We shrink from curves.   Look at our doors and
    windows,
And small straight ugly garden-plots.   I wonder
The curves of trees and girls are not abolished.
    Alouette. Papa, I dreamt they had abolished
    slates . . .
Those dreadful things I have to do my sums upon :
Those *must* be parallelograms.

Astrologos. Space is a cone whose height and breadth are limitless.
The summit God, the base in deep eternities.
Therefore the planet's orbit is elliptical;
Therefore the comet flies in a parabola.
    Alouette (aside). Papa grows conical. I call it comical.

Astrologos. Cut just one link of the great chain centripetal,
And there's an end of the enormous universe.
    Alouette. Tell me which link, papa. I'll get my scissors out.

Astrologos. I have seen men and women, hats and petticoats;
I have seen boys that lived upon pure intellect;
I have seen girls that lived on simple impudence;
Dogs are, I think, superior to humanity.
    Alouette. They don't talk nonsense and conceive it sense, papa.

Alouette. To come of age ! Do all men come
of age, papa,
At the same moment ?
Astrologos. Darling, not a bit of it.
I've known a man who never came of age at all,
Though he was ninety at his death.
I've known a man
Who came of age a baby in his bassinette,
And was a man before he spoke a syllable.

———

Alouette. Papa, I want to know—what *is*
theology ?
It seems to me the hardest of the sciences.
Astrologos. That much depends upon the way
you learn it, child.
I learnt it painfully, from heavy folios :
I let you learn it, being a girl, a feeble thing,
From life of bird and flower, from glowing skies
and seas,
And God's voice whispering in the morn-wind's
melody.
Alouette. To be a feeble girl is some advantage,
then.

———

N

Raphael. How sudden moments spoil the work
of centuries !
Do trifles rule the world ?
Astrologos. In faith, they do, my lord.
A butterfly may overset a dynasty.
A pretty girl may make a realm Republican.
Alouette. A pretty girl's no trifle, you must own,
papa.

———

Astrologos. Pick up your thread.
Alouette. I did not know it fell, papa.
Astrologos. How like a prosy talker, who,
oblivious,
Lets fall his story's thread, and plodding ignorant,
Pursues his wordy way until entanglement
Breaks off his luckless speech.
Alouette. I'm sure such accident
Ne'er happens to a woman's conversation though.

———

The Cardinal. No living man shall dare to
censure me
Save the Holy Father, and he censures not.

What I have done, is done.

Raphael.   Some things are never
Done twice, by the very saintliest of saints :
Your deed is such.

———

Alouette. Papa, the cardinal-legate's sermon
    puzzled me.
Which are the sheep and which the goats, I want
    to know ?
I think a goat upon a mountain pinnacle
Is happier than a sheep in heavy meadow land.
    Astrologos. Heaven's Zodiac hath both Capri-
    corn and Aries.
The spiritual Zodiac is not narrower.

———

Alouette. Surely the Emperor is too old for love,
    papa,
And yet he weds the girlish Countess Isola.
    Astrologos. Hush ! whisper not that Emperors
    can e'er grow old !
At any rate, Love cannot.   In the granite rocks

Fire dwells, and often here are hidden water
    springs,
And the most delicate flowers and mosses cover
    them.

———

Alouette. "The course of true love never did
    run smooth," they say.
I want to know, papa, is false love fortunate?
Astrologos. Of all things on this earth the most
    unfortunate—
Annihilating souls.   False love is hatred, child,
Ἐπίγειος, ψυχική, δαιμονιώδης :
In this the great Apostle of false wisdom spake—
And love is wisdom, or it is not love at all.

———

Alouette. We all of us are kissed beneath the
    mistletoe ;
Kissed by our cousins too, and other wicked ones.
Astrologos. All well enough, before you come
    to womanhood.
But 'tis a very altered matter afterward.
Contact of lips is prelude of a mystery.

———'

Alouette. But who is he, papa ? Is he a Vision,
too ?
Astrologos. He is the Central Vision, dwelling
far away
Where suns are stifled in the Dark intangible,
Where constellations perish like a soap-bubble.
Alouette. What an unpleasant creature !
Astrologos. He's the negative
Father of all things positive.

Alouette. I have been looking at a book of
heraldry :
Papa, please tell me, what's a baton sinister ?
Astrologos. A sign that's made respectable by
Royalty.

Alouette. I've often wished I had Aladdin's
lamp, papa.
Helen of Troy should be my waiting damosel ;
For guardian of my portal should stand Hercules,
Short-haired, with muscles that would split great
trees apart ;

Apollo should make music when I cared for it,
So sweet the world would pause to hear the melody;
If I would swim, a Nereid-nymph should carry
  me ;
If ride, around wise Cheiron's neck my arms should
  cling
While he flew easily through woods of Thessaly ;
And if I cared to fly above the mountain-peaks
Jove's eagle should be summoned as my servitor.

———

Raphael. 'Tis curious that events swing back
  and forward so,   -
With this day merriment and next day misery,
As if it were the swinging of a pendulum.
  Astrologos. It is the swing of Fate's eternal
  pendulum.
See, Charles the Martyr leads to Charles the
  Profligate :
But for the Wesleyans there had been no Puseyites.
  Alouette. And but for wisest sires no silly
  daughters, sir.

———

First ball, first ride to hounds, first radiant opera,
First plunge into the world with all its wickedness
And happiness and agony and poetry ;
First love, first kiss !   O, maddening dreams of
  maidenhood !

Astrologos. You want to know your maddest
  friend—ask Sirius ;
Your wickedest—a Pleiad ran away with him.
Your strongest—take a calm half-hour with Jupiter.
Alouette. The one who loves you best ?
Astrologos. Ask Venus, little one.

Alouette. Father, you never surely knew a
  murderer !
Astrologos. My child, most of our dearest friends
  are murderers :
They murder time and life and wit and oddity,
They murder God in Sabbaths hideous wearisome
They murder poetry by making prose of it,
They murder love in fashionable marriages,

They murder beauty through the odious milliners,
They murder truth in the atrocious newspapers.

Raphael. An oily plausible fellow came, Astro-
    logos,
Up the back stairs by stealth to see me yester-
    day :
Aldiborontiphoscophornio brought him here—
The many-syllabled lordling.
    Astrologos. And his business, Prince ?
    Raphael. To vilify you. To hint that he had
    heard that you
Had done or said or thought things vile and trea-
    sonable,
That your proceedings were by no means ortho-
    dox,
That there were rumours all through Megalopolis
Of your most foul disloyalty and heresy.
    Astrologos. Impalpable dust of slander fills the
    atmosphere,
And blinds the eyes and warps the husky throats
    of men :

But, when truth's sunshaft smites the air, at once
    you see
The small foul atoms of the dirt we tread upon.

Genius is often eaten through with bitterness,
By what may seem a very trifling accident.

See the red tower that rises strong and steadfast
    there,
Holding a dial that tells its tale unceasingly !
Look at the festal halls, the airy terraces,
The great oaks that have grasped the soil for cen-
    turies,
The cedars calm as if they grew on Lebanon,
The lawns as green as laurels in a thunder-shower,
The bright symmetric flower-plots ! Lordly mastiff
    stalks
Over the turf; white pigeons fill the summer air.
A scene more happy than the chief of palaces.
No prince dwells there; only an English gentleman.

An earl of old descent, unbroken pedigree,
A strong and cool and pure and haughty lineage ;
The men all fearless and the women maidenly.
He, climax of a stalwart race, would willingly
Fight fiercely or love madly.   So, love came to
   him.

Wide as the Queen's highway is every corridor ;
In every room there's space to build some cottages ;
You might have races in the picture-gallery.

Let us revivify municipalities :
The good old towns, where men were not ashamed
   of trade,
Nor let trade deaden life or love or strength in
   them,
But fought and conquered in the war of liberty,
And built cathedrals that remain to dwarf our work,
And used keen sword, sweet lyre, the justest
   balances—
Towns such as these the Monarch should resus-
   citate.

A castle dies, when its lord's chivalry perishes ;
A mansion dies, when there's a prosperous rogue
in it ;
A cottage dies, when by sheer scamps inhabited.

Oh, spire of God ! Oh, poem of an architect !
Oh, wondrous winding aisles of saintly mystery !
Prayer blends with praise in this untroubled
solitude.

Raphael. When you are young, a decade makes
a difference.
Astrologos. When you are old, a decade makes
no difference.
Eighty and ninety I consider synonyms :
I have begun to count my age by centuries.

Raphael. Homer wrote nonsense, making gods
and goddesses
Encounter mortals both in bed and battlefield.
These are child's fables.

Astrologos.   Noble Prince, talk warily :
How many senses have you ?
Raphael.   Five.
Astrologos.   I have seven senses.
One gives me power to see things never visible
To you.   This moment I beheld bright ˈIris pass
Over that arch of rainbow that is glittering
From hill to hill.   I have seen brawny Herakles
Foiling an army.   Trust me, your five senses, sir,
Are not the high completion of humanity.

———

Astrologos. You look at life, Prince, through
    rose-tinted spectacles.
Raphael. And you through drab ones.
Astrologos.   Not at all, your Excellence—
I have three sets, with a miraculous difference.
These show the Past, with all its wondrous mys-
    teries ;
Rimmed are they with the horn of the rhinoceros :
These show the Future—rim of gold encircles
    them :
But these, with setting of a very sombre sort,

Mere dusky ebony, my Prince, mere ebony,
Show the strong Present, wheresoever turned they
  are.
Raphael. Go.   May I see my true love?
Astrologos. Take the spectacles.
Raphael. O!

Astrologos. No good was ever done by any
  criminal.
No villainy succeeds.   Cæsars, Iscariots,
Bonapartes, always bring dark doom upon their
  heads.
The law is constant.
Raphael.   I have known some rascals live
Golden delicious lives unkicked.
Astrologos.   Ah, wait a while.
More worlds there are than one, my lord.   They
  know it now.

Raphael. He met *himself,* you say?
Astrologos.   He met himself, my lord,
Creeping to bed along the half-lit corridor,

He met his boy-self, daring, dauntless, devilish,
Poising a rapier with a man's heart's blood on it.
He died that night.

Raphael. But who the devil was my fellow-
traveller?
Astrologos. Speak not too lightly of the devil,
good my lord,
The lowest whisper reaches that great potentate.
Raphael. Being his slave, you fear him, wretched
star-gazer.
He is a dream.

Astrologos.   Nay, good my lord, act warily :
The mad churl's pistol may upset a dynasty.
Raphael. Well, let the dynasty go.   Come, cast
my horoscope,
And you will find that I was born when Jupiter
Just dimmed fair Venus' lovely light at eventide—
Only just dimmed it.

The first Lord of the Admiralty. Prince, we
want millions for a myriad ironclads.
The Chancellor of the Exchequer. Prince, over-
taxing much disgusts the Liberals.
Raphael. What shall I say to all these fiends,
Astrologos ?
Astrologos. Say, *do your business.* Build your
ships to swim and fight ;
Take tax with fairness of the toiling populace ;
Resign your offices, if quite incapable.
Raphael. They *won't* resign.
Astrologos. Because they *are* incapable.

Prince Raphael. Ha ! the new Legate. Has
he power and pertinence ?
Does he seem worthy Hermes of the Vatican ?
Has he the wisdom which befits a cardinal ?
Astrologos. He seems most prudent. I must
cast his horoscope.
Born with the sun in Cancer or in Scorpio,
If I mistake not.

Raphael (*reading a letter*). The Count means well, Astrologos.

Astrologos. Often we find well-meaning men most mischievous.

He means well who means nothing—that's the worst of it—

Who aims to do the right, but cannot see the right,

Whose will is warped by the first gust of circumstance.

Raphael. Friend, have I, save yourself, my tried Astrologos ?

Give me the glory of an honest enemy

Rather than these false friends, false courtiers, servitors.

The fairest friend you have may be untrustworthy ;

The fairest face you see may be a naughty one ;

The fairest life you live may be a broken life.

Raphael. How should men bear their troubles,
O Astrologos ?
Astrologos. Why meet them bravely, Prince;
heroic dauntlessness
Transforms a trouble to a bubble, instantly.

———

Our life is full of mystery, of irony ;
You meet a woman or a man unknown to you,
And all is changed for you through all eternity.

———

Change is the law of all things save the soul of
man,
Which, being divine, is utterly unchangeable.

———

Benedict. She is a daughter of midnight . . .
beautified
In mystery, and in her darkest moods
A creature most bewitching.
Raphael.   Is she so ?

o

Then you are welcome to her witcheries.
I'd rather marry a broomstick, Benedict.
My darling is the daughter of the day,
With eyes like heaven, lips like red roses, speech
Like song of thrush, breath like the summer south,
Touch like the delicate cool grass, and mind
Bright as God's sunshine.

Benedict. A breath, a beauty, a delight, a fan-
    tasy,
A creature that's half hornet and half butterfly . . .
You have seen such.
Raphael.   Ay, and they are not innocent.
This gay young thing is innocent and beautiful ;
She is all butterfly—a flower with wings to her—
A bit of sunrise with a soul.

Alix. She is a very wicked girl, I am sure of it.
I will not speak to her again or think of her.
Raphael. Pshaw, sister ; why the child is just
    as innocent
As you were when . . .

Alix.　　　　　　When what ?

Raphael.　　　　　When God created you ;
Or when my fellow-student, Roderic, looked at you.

Alix.　　　　　　Can men change ?
Women alone I thought were changeable.
You tell us that we vary every hour,
Ay, every minute.

Raphael.　　　　So you do, my sweet :
And 'tis your rarest charm.　Thus fair flowers
　　change
With every warm kiss of the summer sun.
Man changes only once, and then for ever.

Alix. See, see, the great procession moves and
　　winds
Like some strange many-coloured serpent, winding
Along the astonished road.　But who is that,
Dark-clothed, gray-haired, erect upon his steed,
With eyes that seem to see another world,
Passing this pageant by ?

Raphael.   The Earl, my own :
He hath no care for pageants.

Alix. A house of statesmen, soldiers, scholars,
    poets,
Since they first bred.
Raphael.   Ay, and of lovers, darling ;
The man will never help the state, nor lead
Armies to victory, nor teach the world
With scholar's mastery or poet's fire,
Unless he has loved.
Alix.   And won ?
Raphael.   Or lost, mayhap.

Would you have music ?   Listen to a waterfall.
The scale is infinite, and God is organist.

Life's highway has a million curious travellers ;
The pure bride elbowed by the wretched courtesan;
The poet by a statesman or a pickpocket ;
The gentle man by fellows self-styled gentlemen.

London is hard to villagers and voyagers,
Being an aggregate of myriad villages,
Being a human ocean where the voyager
Is sore perplexed by longitude and latitude.

———

I lived, I loved, I lingered in the country, till
The great green woods became an awful agony,
The long still roads unutterable weariness ;
And then I said, " A little fool my sweetheart is ;
She loves not me ; she only loves herself—I guess
I'll go and see if London beats the villages."

———

" God was first gardener and Cain first citizen :"
So says an English poet, a forgotten one.

———

Void is the man of what befits a gentleman,
Void of the English easy humorous courtesy,
Void of the pure contempt for dull rascality,
Void utterly of Christ's unmeasured kindliness,
Void of high feeling, and a trifle viperous.

———

Astrologos. He is where never any birds shall
fly to him,
Nor any melody of summer meet his ear,
Nor any message enter, any issue thence
To tell a word of him.
Raphael.   All fiends are pitiless ;
The imperial Fiend is of all fiends most merciless.

Astrologos. Ambition has, my lord, unknown
developments,
And when a man has squeezed the sponge of life
enough
To satisfy the multitude, he yearns once more
For something utterly beyond the multitude,
Something immeasurable, mad, impossible.
Raphael. With such a man, I have the strongest
sympathy :
My sorrow is, to me there's nought impossible.
Alouette (aside). Make love to me, fair Prince,
and see what comes of it.

Raphael. You are full of foolish fancies, Alouette:
You never could have seen that man before.
   Alouette. Oh, have I not? Oh, he was my one
   terror
When I was quite a baby, in my dreams.
I had forgotten those dread dreams, I had,
Till this grim gaunt old monster came to-day,
Just as polite as ever, just as horrid.

   Astrologos. Nothing is half so glorious as a
   thunderstorm.
   Alouette. O yes, papa, a thunderstorm is exquisite,
If you have only some one's arm around your
   waist.

   Alouette. Some one to love, papa. Yes, that's
   the wish I have.
Some one with whom to listen to the nightingales
When they are singing old delicious love stories ;
Some one to watch me as I slumber quietly,
And perhaps disturb my dreams with just a kiss
   or two.

Astrologos. Girls are such fools.   Some one to
   plague and worry you,
Some one to take advantage of your weaknesses,
Some one to make a silly little slave of you.

Astrologos. You say that you're in love, you
   little reprobate ?
Alouette. In love !   Of course.   What *do* men
   bring up daughters for,
Except to love ?   The cat must have its mice, you
   know,
And when a kitten watches at the wainscoting
The unfledged bird, whose wings are rudimentary
(A favourite word of yours, papa !) desires to fly.
   Astrologos. And often topples from the nest
   and breaks its neck.

Alouette. You really mean it, Prince ?
Raphael. Of course I mean it, love.
Soon shall you hear the bridal prothalamion
That hints sweet marvels of the happy marriage-bed,

And you will blush amid the maids, a ruddy rose.
Hearing the soft lute whisper wondrous witchery.
 Astrologos. Why should she blush, my Prince?
 The light of Hesper,
Sad passionate Sappho's star, brings nought more
 life-giving
Than love.
 Alouette. Ay me! as if I had not life enough.
I want no star of eve to cheer me, Raphael:
I only want a lover, gay and chivalrous,
Who will shed starsheen on the dullest eventide.
 Raphael. You have him, beauty. What care
 we for Hesperus?

 Raphael. Well, Alouette, where shall we pass
 our honeymoon?
Shall we see cities? Shall we chase the marvellous
Beauty of mountains? Shall we hide in forest
 depths?
Where shall we go to get most lovely loneliness?
 Alouette. We'll go to sea.

Alouette. I like the sea, Prince.

Raphael.   Yes, the flying yacht, you know.
With topmast royals, making timber perilous,
And a gay wind to race with !

Alouette.   Ah, but plunge in it !
Down in the depths cool your hot eyes with emerald
Wave made for mermaids !   Fathom the abysses
     where
Strange creatures dwell—a world unknown, un-
     knowable—
Perhaps a race more great than men can ever be !

O little love, whose lightest line is beautiful . . .
The brightest dewdrop on the rose that's ruddiest !

A LETTER TO THE
RIGHT HON. B. DISRAELI, M.P.

1869.

Born Tories to astound and Whigs to enrage,
Yours the chief name of the Victorian age,
Disraeli ! You have learnt this realm to sway,
Prophetic of yourself in *Vivian Grey*.
In no respect I envy your career—
A genius servile to a brilliant peer ;
Destined defender of a falling Church,
Which her sworn sons are leaving in the lurch ;
Destined to fight for all that you despise,
Leading to sure disaster troops unwise.
What cruel fate, young genius to appal,
Has made you very great and very small ?
Great, in keen scheme and stratagem oblique ;
Small, in subservience to a torpid clique ?
You have been Minister ; with inward scorn
Have tossed his strawberry leaves to Abercorn ;

Have borne as colleagues statecraft's weakest
  sons,
Walpoles and Hardys, Northcotes, Pakingtons ;
Have made peers, bishops, judges, quite a
  swarm—
And thunderstruck the Commons with reform.

Now on the left hand bench you sit apart,
While autocratic as a Bonaparte,
Gladstone to victory leads the Liberal race,
And talks of justice while he thinks of place.
You never claimed on moral ground respect,
But simply rested on your intellect,
And safe the basis, for, while earth endures,
Few men will have such intellect as yours ;
But Gladstone with the world severely quarrels,
Unless we all admit his rigorous morals ;
The man is truly good and truly pious
(Though never was a bowl without a bias),
And when he does the most destructive deeds,
Upon the highest principle proceeds ;
Ay, while defeat the wicked Tory hardens,
Prays for his enemy in Carlton Gardens.

BULLIED by Gladstone and perplexed by you,
What will the blatant bleating Commons do?
Upon Reform such time and talk were spent,   '
Men hoped to see a People's Parliament.
What is the truth? The old old story still—
Wide-incomed Smith beats narrow-minded Mill.
Brewers and bankers, men of odious omen,
Auriferous fellows of immense abdomen,
Flashy directors, with their diamond rings—
Such are the mass of our six hundred kings.
What care they for the people? What care they
In mind and body though the poor decay,
Perish for lack of bread and lack of light,
Life a dull toil and death eternal night?
Once Bright the souls of ministers dismayed—
Now Bright blots foolscap at the Board of Trade;
To the official tone his voice inclines,
A burly giant of the Philistines.
Who now, within St. Stephen's guarded door,
Forgets his party, speaking for the poor?
Who represents the working classes here?
Ayrton, whose loftiest effort is a sneer,
Or stingy Fawcett, who would fain be free
To take his place without an entrance-fee?

No ; there is none to help the poor.   They wait
As in old times outside the well-barred gate.
This was their Parliament, so people said :
With what strange swiftness has the fancy fled !
Highly respectable are all who sit
In that abode of wisdom and of wit ;
Men of warm wealth, whose daughters go to
    Court,
Who dine profusely, and are fond of port.
What if the House had held a Beales or two ?
Beales would have dined and drunk his sloe-juice
    too.
While " rascal counters " give of seats a choice,
How shall the blind sad people find a voice ?

" Nay, look at Gladstone," cries a Liberal friend,
" His the clear intellect, the glorious end,
His the unsullied and unselfish mind—
One of the angels left by chance behind."
Glad would I welcome the seraphic guest,
This Aristides, better than the best.
But while he fights the battle of the creeds,
Wholly forgotten are the nation's needs ;

The ignorance, and penury, and crime,
The unutterable trouble of the time,
The woe of millions—what are these to him ?
He wins his place and gratifies a whim,
The Irish parsons of their money tricks,
And gives the gold to Irish lunatics.
What odds ! In Ireland, if we credit fame,
Parson and lunatic are much the same.

HE who shall come to show this realm the way
To perfect freedom, is not here to-day.
You, sir, by sufferance who served the Queen—
You are not he, whate'er you might have been.
Yet when, quite tired of wit, I turn away
From ebrious fantasies of *Vivian Grey*,
And rest awhile on *Sybil's* shadowy page,
I think sometimes you understand this age ;
Still it were vain your projects to expand,
Since you this age can never understand.

THE statesman comes not : will the poet come ?
Since Byron died, the Muses have been dumb.

Wordsworth was great, you tell me. Yes, of course;
But Byron was an elemental force—
Not an Apollo, such as Stratford sees,
But a fierce dauntless fighting Hercules ;
English in brain and fibre, power and pique—
(Browning's Italian, and the Laureate Greek).
English that epic in the octave rhyme,
On whose wide canvas he has sketched the time :
English the wild eccentric course he ran—
He was a poet . . . ay, and more, a man.

Is Tennyson no poet ?   Yes, indeed,
" Miss Alfred's " are delicious books to read :
In summer tide, when all the woods are still,
Pleasant to wander at one's own sweet will,
Dream of the amorous gossiping that broke
The eternal silence of a garrulous oak,
Dream of the Princess who was buried deep
In an unfathomed century of sleep,
Dream of the savage adjectives that fall
From the loud lunatic of *Locksley Hall.*
Sweet singer of the madrigal melodious
Why did he make King Arthur's story odious ?

Why, with a flattery at which men wince,
Compare the hero to a blameless Prince ?
Why send the old figures to a modern school,
Turn Vivian harlot, Merlin sensual fool ?

LOVELY and lucid are the Laureate's pearls :
A perfect poet, sir, for little girls.
Soft flows his rhymeless verse, constructed well,
And sweetly matched each soothing syllable.
But where's the passion a great poet knows
When the hot blood in every artery flows ?
Not his the satire even fools can feel,
When each strong line is a keen blade of steel ;
Not his the lyric love that has unlaced
The cestus, warm from Aphrodite's waist ;
But if you like a smooth Virgilian style,
A very proper moral, free from bile,
Ethics of Dr. Watts', Colenso's creed,
Those nice green volumes give you all you need.

GREATER and less is Browning : greater far
He will be, dwelling in some future star.

P

This world's his nursery : well we know his tune—
A baby-giant, crying for the moon.
If he were only English ! if he could
But think in English it would do him good.
Now, in Italian subtlety immersed,
His last and longest poem is his worst ;
He tells a tale whose actors would delight
Charles Reade or Wilkie Collins, men of might,
A tale the Adelphi would receive with joy—
And makes it longer than the tale of Troy.

ARNOLD is English.   On the Berkshire marge
Of Thames, I see him watch the tardy barge,
While the swift swallow in endless cycle flies,
While the scythed hay in swathes of summer lies.
Ah ! and he muses, wandering thus alone,
On one pure spirit, now in realms unknown.
Has that true poet, quick-departing guest,
In other regions found perpetual rest ?
I can forgive who saw the Reveller stray
To where Odysseus in Aiaie lay—
Who watched the Gipsy Scholar's mazy path
Over wild wold and solitary strath—

I can forgive him, that mysterious haze
Shrouds every vision of his later days,
That life is lost in melancholy mist . . .
But why the deuce did he turn essayist ?

SWINBURNE, a singer perfect as the birds,
Poet spontaneous, demigod of words,
Too fond, no doubt, of blood and filth and foam,
With the hetaira far too much at home,
Yet rises to the height of the highest bard,
Pourtraying Mary with her Chastelard.
Learned historians, prodigies of toil,
Ne'er touched his picture of the Harlot Royal.
They could not know her chamber's faint perfume,
Or how lamps flickered in that amorous room,
Or how she kissed, or how white throat and breast
Throbbed through the midnight's exquisite unrest,
Or how her serpent nature, sensuous, cruel,
Made of what men call love a deadly duel—
Wherein the opponent always fell we know,
Dauphin or Darnley, Bothwell, Rizzio.
Heartless and shameless, perfect form and face,
The poison-blossom of the Stuart's wild race,

Knowledge of her was Swinburne's fame and fate :
Behold, I crown him Mary's Laureate.

NOTHING I know, and nothing will I say,
Of Morris—Chaucer of the modern day :
Thus much I learn from various reviews—
He's husband now of Chaucer's widowed Muse.
Of Locker what ?   Apollo in the fashion—
Humour and pathos mild, no touch of passion.
From Suckling, Lovelace, Prior, Luttrel, Praed,
Locker inherits his inspiring Maid :
Not nude and passionate, not fast and flighty,
Like Swinburne's rosy-bosomed Aphrodite :
Not icy cold as Parian sculpture is,
Like Tennyson's blue-stockinged Artemis :
Not erudite and sapient, grimly frowning,
Like the Athena that's adored by Browning :
But just the Period's Girl, a pretty creature,
Of dainty style though inexpressive feature,
Who carefully reserves her choice opinions
For length of petticoats and bulk of chignons,
In whom no tragic impulse ever rankles,
Who always says her prayers and shows her ankles.

THREE needs are ours amid this century's
    whirl . . .
The ideal Politician, Poet, Girl.
What of the statesman ? His keen eye should
    see
The visionary future of the free ;
That wondrous epoch in the days to come
In whose broad light debaters shall be dumb,
When Kings shall rest on something more than
    morals,
And even Bishops shall refrain from quarrels,
When wealth and titles shall be little prized,
And manhood—God's own likeness—recognised.
Believing in that time—O glorious creed,
Even though the nations never should be freed !
Our statesman's task must be to force the door
Which shuts from happiness the mean and poor.
Churches and railways, trade's unchecked ad-
    vance,
Projects of Prussia, interests of France,
The Yankee Commonwealth's insane ambitions !
Such things engage our living politicians.
Mere trash and chaff, green ferret and red tape,
Foolscap to crown the pert official ape ! ,

You, strong triumvirate, Gladstone, Bright, and
    Lowe,
Are millions of our people brutes or no ?
Can you arrange the future of the masses . . .
Control the dangerous, desperate, devilish classes ?
Of course we know old England's staying power :
But there may come too terrible an hour,
Too fierce a flame for orators and prigs,
For prelates, landed gentry, moderate Whigs,
Hotter than Greys and Russells can endure,
Or the Gladstonian patent nostrums cure :
In fact a revolution in the air,
A popular earthquake . . . *and no Cromwell there.*

As to the Poet : Critics may upbraid—
I think a Poet's should not be a trade :
I don't care much to see Apollo's oxen
Herded through Dover Street by muddling Moxon.
My notion of a poet is, you know,
Valerius of Verona, long ago . . .
Passionate poet and consummate metrist,
Who hymned the sparrow on his Lesbia's sweet
    wrist,

Who loved and uttered love with lyric cry
(Not for the drachmæ of the Sosii),
Whose swift phaselus dared the distant seas,
Who caught the mad song of the Mænades,
Whose vigorous verse smote Cæsar like a sword.
Such was Catullus.   Now the world is bored
With gentlemen who manufacture rhyme,
And by a tramway their Parnassus climb.
Men whose blood stagnates in their puffy veins,
Who pick their words, and take elaborate pains.
While your true poet like the eagle flies
Through blue abysses of untravelled skies,
Scathes the gross tyrant and his slaves with scorn,
And hails the crimson of earth's coming morn.

THE Lady of the Future, who can paint?
She will not be a sinner or a saint,
Will not o'erflow with Ritualistic bile,
Or imitate too closely Phryne's style.
Who cares for either of them, first or last,
The girl who fasts, the girl who is rather fast?
O to bring back the great Homeric time,
The simple manners and the deeds sublime:

When the wise Wanderer, often foiled by Fate,
Through the long furrow drave the ploughshare
    straight,
When Nausicaa, lovely as a dream,
Washed royal raiment in the shining stream !
Such men, such maidens, are the sort we seek :
Can English blood produce them like the Greek ?

THE END.

Printed by R. & R. CLARK, *Edinburgh.*